FEROCIOUS

FEROCIOUS

HELLCAT RELEASED™ BOOK FOUR

MICHAEL ANDERLE

LMBPN Publishing
PMB 196, 2540 South Maryland Pkwy
Las Vegas, NV 89109

Version 1.00, August 2022
ebook ISBN: 979-8-88541-733-4
Print ISBN: 979-8-88541-734-1

THE FEROCIOUS TEAM

Thanks to the JIT Readers

Dave Hicks
Diane L. Smith
Christopher Gilliard
Zacc Pelter
Dorothy Lloyd

If I've missed anyone, please let me know!

Editor
The SkyFyre Editing Team

DEDICATION

To Family, Friends and
Those Who Love
to Read.
May We All Enjoy Grace
to Live the Life We Are
Called.

— Michael

CHAPTER ONE

Dante Shale stood on the interior deck of the shuttle, about ten feet from the side gate. In the next minute, it would open to dump him and his companions into the frozen wastes of the planet known as Earth.

Beside him to the left, Braelin Klement, one of his three new apprentices, quipped, "Why the hell don't any of the Stations have a climate like this? I mean, it perks a man up, right? Makes him feel alive and shit."

Dante stared straight ahead with his intense green gaze. "Unless it kills him first. Most people seem to prefer having everything climate-controlled." He loosened himself up and shrugged into his heavy coat, gloves, and hood, getting a feel for how it would affect his mobility. Most of it he wore atop his armor, but its thickness meant it could still get in the way of his ability to run, jump, climb, stab, or shoot.

"Typical," Braelin scoffed. "I don't know. I'm looking forward to a nice change of pace." A tremor went through his small frame. His twinkling eyes and short, silver-tinged beard were faintly visible under the protective hood he wore over his helmet.

By now, Dante knew the man well enough to grasp that

joking around and making inane comments was his way of trying to relieve tension before something big happened.

For him, today's job was about as big as it got. It would be the first day he and the other two accompanied their boss on a Dirt-side mission.

Opposite Braelin on Dante's right was the second apprentice, Jolo Neburu. A tall, slim, and strikingly elegant woman with deep ebony skin, she held herself poised in silence, taking in everything that happened around her but declining to comment on it. Despite her relative quiet, there was something magnetic about her. She could not help drawing attention anywhere she went, even from people who were used to her presence.

Braelin asked her, "Hey, Jolo. What was the average temperature at your Station?"

She smiled in an understated sardonic way, faintly amused. "Enough."

Braelin laughed but didn't push her for further details. Instead, he checked the controls on his pulsecore carbine for the fourth or fifth time.

Nasreen Joelle steered the shuttle as close to the ice as possible without causing major disruption to the craft or landscape. The thrusters were less powerful in hover mode, but they still put out enough heat to melt through the ice sheet, so the four Marauders would have to jump from a higher distance than usual.

"Okay," Nasreen called. "This is as low as I can go without burning a hole through the ice into the sea. Good luck out there. I'll be in communication if you need anything."

Their headsets were all tuned to the same frequency as the shuttle's communications system. Dante liked having a dedicated comms person plus a dedicated pilot, but Nasreen was capable of handling both by herself.

He breathed in. "Open it, then. I'll go first."

The hatch in front of him rose, and beyond it lay a deep,

frosty nighttime darkness that extended for hundreds of miles. There was little to see besides the black clouds and the faint wisps of dust blowing over the vast expanse of ice on the frigid wind. Once, the North Sea had remained unfrozen for much of the year. No longer. The planet's weather patterns had irrevocably altered since the calamity that drove humankind into orbit.

Dante did one final quick check of his gear—his armor, his supply packs, and the heavy rifle he held in his grasp. Normally he preferred lighter, more compact weapons, but they had reason to expect stiffer resistance than usual. Braelin and Neburu had more standard carbines loaded with explosive pulsecore rounds. Usually such weapons were more than sufficient for all but the most overwhelming odds.

Satisfied that everything was in order, he grabbed the bungee cord attached to the hull and jumped out into the void beyond the hatch.

The expected dizzying, sickening sensation filled him as he plummeted, then the cord tightened and slowed his fall. They had measured it close to perfect. The sheen of meltwater became apparent as he drew closer to the ice, and his descent became a drift rather than a fall. Still, when his boots struck the surface, there was enough force in the impact that he rolled to neutralize it, released the cord, and came out of the motion kneeling as the bungee shot back up to the shuttle.

Dante got to his feet and performed a hasty visual scan of the surrounding landscape. Nothing showed nearby except the frozen ocean's irregular but mostly flat expanse. Here and there a few icebergs had been trapped within the crust, forming random hills, cliffs, and mountains amid the makeshift landscape.

To the east, he vaguely made out the silhouette of the abandoned Norwegian oil rig. Their destination and target. It had been a highly advanced facility in its day. If their client's hopes proved fruitful, its computers still held long-lost software that could revolutionize the modern robotics industry.

Dante turned and looked back at the hovering shuttle. To his total lack of surprise, the next crewmember out was his third apprentice, Mugoi.

Mugoi had originally been a human being, probably a man, although no one was quite certain. It now preferred to be called "it" but was willing to tolerate "he." It was roughly humanoid in appearance, but judging its exact nature was a difficult task. The cybernetic organism was a product of the growing cult of transhumanism, an unusually extreme one.

Mugoi leapt out the door, hands clinging to the cord. Its movements were perfect, perhaps too perfect. The numerous augmentations it had enhanced its reflexes beyond what most human beings were capable of.

As the robotic form slid toward the ice, Dante reflected on another cyborg he had known a year ago. Eduardo H. Curtidor, more commonly known as Mr. Hyde. Like Mugoi, he'd had most of his body replaced by advanced tech. In Hyde's case, the difference could not be starker.

Hyde had been a huge, lumbering, clanking thing powered by hydraulics who moved with a jerky stiffness and relied on brute force and intimidation. Mugoi was a sleek, dexterous, androgynous being with perfectly sculpted features and a body optimized for graceful movement. It lacked Hyde's raw power, but Mugoi's strength was still considerable. Greater than its size would suggest.

Mugoi's feet touched the ice with a deft lightness that required no roll. The cyborg simply squatted and stood straight, releasing the cord. "That was not so bad," it said in its soft, harmonious voice.

"Right," Dante agreed. "Be ready in case anyone else needs help."

Mugoi smiled and nodded. He checked his weapons, a pair of pistols loaded with advanced-penetrator drill rounds. They didn't make as obvious a mess as pulsecores did but were still extremely deadly in the hands of a skilled user.

It was tough to be sure, but Dante had long had the faint impression that the cyborg regarded the other two apprentices not merely as companions but as competitors. He often chose tools, weapons, and combat roles that differed from the others. He wanted to distinguish himself as much as possible.

Braelin was next, then Neburu. Neither had any trouble, but Braelin landed harder and faster than he wanted and gritted his teeth in pain after rolling across the ice.

He held up his hands in protest while Neburu rappelled down behind him. "No, no, I'm fine," he insisted. "Only the usual aches and pains. Why the hell am I going through all this reeducation stuff at my age, anyway?"

Dante responded, "That's a question you have to answer your-self. If anything, we're the ones who are supposed to ask it."

Braelin was only a few years older than Dante. It made him realize that his career as a Plunderer was not something he could do forever. Everyone aged and died unless they went the same route as Hyde and Mugoi.

The cyborg watched with calm satisfaction as Braelin struggled, taking in the sight for a second or two before helping the middle-aged man up.

Neburu landed then. She also fell into a roll but sprang up from it in top form. She had plenty of experience as a fighter and was still in the prime of life.

Dante looked the three over. "All right, so far, so good. I don't think we're going to be alone out here for much longer. Especially since intel suggests the rig is crawling with Nightmutts. No itchy trigger fingers. We don't want to damage the merchandise. If you *have* to shoot, don't hesitate."

At that, a voice in Dante's head spoke. *"The rig is still host to a number of those bear-like creatures as of the most recent satellite data. Several aquatic lifeforms are approaching our position under the ice."*

Dante frowned but nodded. The voice of a cultured British

gentleman belonged to Midas, the AI chip module he'd had implanted within his skull.

"Yeah," he muttered. "Thanks, Midas. Keep us updated with anything important. Otherwise, try to keep silent. You know how it is."

"Of course, sir. I'll be standing by."

The apprentices were accustomed to listening to Dante's conversations seemingly with himself. AI implants were not *that* uncommon. Midas could speak aloud through a voice module, but he typically did not. Instead, he interfaced directly with Dante's brain.

The quartet moved out, tramping across the ice toward the oil rig. The structure seemed even more massive as it grew closer. The amount of ice that encased its lower reaches had increased its apparent bulk. No one was sure when the North Sea had frozen over or if it had thawed and refrozen, but the rig had been inoperable for many years.

Dark silhouettes crowded around its base and mounted on its walls were starting to move.

The intensely cold wind had yet to penetrate. The team's thick hooded coats blocked most of it, and their armor produced a small amount of heat they could turn inward in frigid conditions. Nonetheless, a slight chill ran through Dante's body.

In his many years as a Marauder, excavating valuable materials from all over the ruined Earth, he had encountered a wide variety of Nightmutts. Virtually all were the stuff of nightmares. When the planet's damaged core had begun to induce mutations, it sometimes seemed like it had been following a plan devised by some evil god or mad scientist.

In this case, things Dante had dubbed "yeti-bears" dominated the local fauna above the ice and giant spider-crabs below. He was not looking forward to meeting either species up close. At least they weren't Dirtwalkers.

Neburu remarked, "There are a great many of them, I see."

Her long fingers moved over the smooth surface of her pulsecore carbine in anticipation.

"Correct," Dante confirmed.

Braelin groaned. "Why did we take this job again? Oh wait, the *fun* of it. And the money, of course. Plenty of that."

Dante had a longstanding tendency to answer people's bullshit questions in a blunt, direct manner. In some cases he didn't realize they were joking, but in others, he simply couldn't be bothered to pretend.

"Because I want all three of you together on a dangerous mission. Think of it as your final exam. If you guys can pull through on this, I'll know that I didn't make a mistake in taking you under my wing."

He was confident in them. Still, his words implied they could fail to live up to that same confidence.

Before anyone could say more, he added, "Oh, and because Nasreen and I are trying to get along better with our earthbound cousins. Most Dirtwalkers would rather not get killed because people like us come out of the sky to steal things from under them. We're trying to lean toward jobs that *aren't* in heavily populated areas, especially not if they'll jeopardize Dirtwalkers' livelihoods or are likely to provoke confrontations."

Braelin responded at once. "Oh. Right, forgot about that. So we end up in the most godforsaken place on Earth, more or less."

Mugoi chuckled. "What better place to test ourselves? I'm sure we *all* can handle it, Braelin."

The small man grumbled but stopped complaining. They were almost within firing distance of the creatures huddled around the oil rig's base. Water sloshed, and via a brief flash of moonlight that slipped between the dark cloud cover, Dante glimpsed what the Nightmutts were doing.

A group of the yeti-bears pulled some of the swarming spider-crabs through a hole in the ice to tear them apart and eat them. Their shells *crunched* between the larger monsters' powerful jaws. It looked like one of the bears had been mortally wounded by the crabs' pincers. It lay dead or dying near the edge of the hole. While the other bears were distracted, a swarm of the spidery aquatic beasts rose from the waves and pulled the furry body under to return the favor. The two species relied upon one another for their food.

Neburu asked, "Can we get past them without shooting?"

Dante grunted. "Doubtful. We'll disperse them long enough to get onto the rig. Then we have to watch our backs. They won't stay scared for long. Not when food is potentially involved."

Nasreen's voice sounded in their headsets. "I might be able to frighten some of them away by flying closer to the rig, but there's a risk of the thrusters damaging the ice or the rig itself, so let's save that option for if we need it. Over."

"Agreed. We'll let you know. Out."

He turned to his apprentices. "This is where the real shit begins, ladies, gentlemen, and others. I expect peak performance from each of you and will be watching. The fewer mistakes you make, the better—and if you make one, *learn from it*. Let's start with a volley directed over there to see how those things react to the noise."

He aimed his rifle and fired a .50 caliber slug at a large chunk of protruding ice about seven feet to the right edge of the rig's base. The gun's report was like thunder. The team's headsets neutralized the worst of the noise, but its extreme loudness was still obvious. The ice chunk exploded, scattering chips all around.

The hulking, shaggy forms of the yeti-bears convulsed with shock and horror and let out a chorus of bestial howls and roars. Braelin and Neburu opened up with their pulsecore carbines, firing at much the same spot. The miniature plasma rounds popped against the ice, raising brief flashes of green light and cracking the surface to expose the saltwater below. Two yeti-bears blundered into the barrage, which ripped them apart. The others fled.

Mugoi aimed his two pistols and squeezed off half a dozen shots from each, aiming at the bears' posteriors. The one in the rear fell, perforated with bleeding holes, but otherwise, he only contributed to scaring the others off.

Dante smirked. "Good. They'll be back shortly. Also, Neburu, you pulled the trigger twice on an empty magazine instead of keeping an eye on your shot counter HUD and reloading in time."

She scowled, ejected the mag, and slapped in a new one. "Forgive me."

"Forgive yourself, but avoid doing it again. Move in. Those crabs don't seem as spooked as the bears were. Be ready to waste them if you have to."

They all trotted across the ice. The coating of dust atop the makeshift ground and the sharp treads of their boots gave them decent traction. In places where water had broken through the surface or where the pulsecore explosions had melted some of it, their footing became too slippery to move as fast as they'd like. They made their way toward a broad security ladder meant for use by personnel who might have fallen into the ocean in the old days before the mass freezing.

Mugoi moved out in front as some of the crabs, which resembled hideous blue spiders the size of large dogs, crept out of the sea to scuttle toward them. "I'll handle this," he purred and peppered the creatures with drill rounds from his handguns.

Three or four crabs out in front spewed ichor from their punctured shells. Their long legs thrashed as they curled up to die. The others finally took the hint and retreated, huddling against the base of the oil rig as the four humans climbed to the main platform.

Once they reached it, Braelin moved out along the edge, only to be caught by a gust of wind that pushed him toward a slick spot of frost. His boot connected with it and slipped. He gyrated wildly and had to stomp his other foot against a beam to avoid falling over the edge. Neburu was nearby and tried to grab his sleeve, but he steadied himself in time.

Dante frowned. "Klement, always be sure of your footing before charging out, especially when clearing corners on uncertain surfaces."

"Sorry, boss." He exhaled and adjusted his helmet. "Should have known better."

Dante waved it off. "Yes, you should have, but at least now you know why it's important. Move out."

They crossed the platform toward a cabin attached to the rig's tower-like central part that contained the drilling apparatus. More important to their mission was the network mainframe. Hopefully, the sought-after robotics software was still intact and awaiting retrieval.

The elements threatened them on their short dash across the rig. The wind had picked up, and the rig was high enough for airspeed to increase noticeably. Decades of harsh exposure without maintenance had caused parts of the platform to sag or collapse. Dante narrowly avoided a weak beam underfoot, hopping to the side as it fell away from the rig and crashed into the ice below.

His gaze snapped up. "Mugoi, you crossed this spot a second ago. Next time, warn everyone else about a treacherous patch of footing."

"Understood." The cyborg was competitive enough that although criticism irked him, he usually took it to heart and rarely made the same mistake twice.

Behind and around them, out on the frozen sea, ungainly shapes were starting to reconverge on the rig. Not only were the yeti-bears who'd been scared off returning, but more of them from nearby had come to investigate the commotion.

Dante urged, "We need to do this fast. Blow the hinges off the cabin door. We don't have time to fuck around with doing it the gentle way."

Braelin fired a single pulsecore round at the door's handle area. It detonated against the steel and sent out a piece of shrapnel that ricocheted off Braelin's shoulder pad but otherwise melted it. The door swung open and sagged off its hinges in time for Mugoi to charge in at the head of the group. Neburu and Dante followed with Braelin taking the rear.

The hallway continued to angle down, and by the time they reached the bent, half-functional door at the end, Dante feared they were at or beneath sea level. Which meant that their target might well be frozen within the ice. Or, worse still, trapped in the deadly black waters beneath it.

Writing, presumably in Norwegian, was plastered across the warped metal of the door. Midas translated. *"Control room. That would be the place, sir."*

"Thanks." Dante tapped the side of his head. "Okay, everyone stand back. I'm kicking the door in, and if that doesn't work we'll have to blast it. Either way, once it's open, everyone fan out within. Stay in formation. Trigger discipline, no covering anyone else with your muzzles. Got it?"

In unison, they replied in the affirmative. Dante rushed forward and slammed his boot hard against the weakest part of the door, where the metal had bent near the frame, and he could see through a gap beyond it.

The door did not give way at the first kick, but it loosened enough while groaning. He figured a second or third would do the trick. His next kick snapped something important, and the entire door fell off its frame inward, disclosing an irregular portal that opened onto a square catwalk.

Mugoi dashed out in front with his pistols ready, covering the space ahead of them while Braelin and Neburu came up behind him and aimed their carbines around his flanks.

Dante snapped, "Klement, try to stay lower. Also, remember to keep an eye on what's below the catwalk."

Braelin coughed. "Yes, sir. Doesn't seem to be much. At least, not anything alive."

Neburu added, "If we make too much commotion, those crab things will notice and swarm in here under the ice."

Mugoi chuckled. "Under the ice is where we must go. Look." He pointed down.

The main network assembly, which presumably contained the console they would need to download the rig's pertinent software, was mostly submerged. The ice sheet had enveloped it at an angle, and its lower reaches were probably within the water. The schematics Dante had examined earlier suggested the most sensitive equipment had waterproofing as a security measure, but decades of submersion might have taken their toll.

Dante looked down at the console and grimaced while his companions moved out to the sides along the catwalk. "Damn. We need to power up the network assembly, which will require breaking the ice. Then someone will have to dive into that water to hook up a portable generator. There won't be any juice left in this rig after all these years. Priming the auxiliary is on us."

Each of them had a generator in their backpack. Their armor was mostly waterproof. The sheer coldness of the depths below the ice would make hypothermia a real threat.

Neburu commented, "We will have to be quick. Again, the crabs will come as soon as the ice shatters. I should be able to handle it."

"Or I," Braelin pointed out. "After all, I'm the expendable one, right?"

Mugoi came up next to Neburu. "Excuse me. May I see your pulsecore?"

Dante watched as the cyborg gently took the carbine from the woman, who looked skeptical but didn't object. Then, abruptly, he fired three shots down over the catwalk into the frozen crust beneath them, the miniature explosions cracking the ice away from the assembly console. Black water sloshed up around it.

"Mugoi!" Neburu exclaimed. "We aren't ready to—"

Mugoi shoved the gun back into her hands and dove over the railing, turning into a humanoid harpoon as he pierced the water's surface and vanished under it. A moment later, he resurfaced next to the console.

Braelin whistled. "He always has to show off, doesn't he? Or it, whatever."

A flustered Neburu looked around. "I hear something. The crabs are already moving this way."

Dante went to the railing and leaned over it. "Hurry up, Mugoi." He did not say it aloud, but he was grateful that the transhumanist had cut off the squabbling between the apprentices over who would have the honor of risking their life. They didn't have time for pointless arguments of that sort.

Mugoi pulled a generator from his pack, clung to the assembly with one hand, and planted the device near the power supply. He switched it on. It lit up and hummed, and to everyone's relief, glowing lights came on throughout the network machinery and the overhead lights of the control room. Their helmet visors adjusted to the surge in brightness, disclosing a surprisingly pristine chamber despite all the damage it had taken and the many years of being abandoned.

Midas spoke. *"The network is functional! I'm searching for the relevant files and ought to be able to download them directly. If by some chance I can't, we'll have to extract the hard drive, which should be possible if I can get the blueprints to the mainframe."*

Below, Mugoi squatted atop a power box, pistols in hand, the water glistening off his artificial skin. It sounded like the crabs were getting closer.

Dante breathed in slowly. "If you can't download it, we may not have time for the hard-copy version."

"Well, I've barely started. As long as we remain in this chamber long enough, there should be no—"

Neburu cried, "The bear-things are coming down the hall!"

Dante looked up. The creatures had managed to surprise them all. As predators, they were capable of great stealth when stalking their prey, even if they reverted to pure savagery once they were in range. The massive hairy beasts filled the doorway before him. His heart leapt into his throat as the first one charged.

CHAPTER TWO

Dante barely had time to aim. He fired two rounds as soon as his rifle's muzzle pointed in the general direction of the hallway leading back out of the control room.

The heavy gun *boomed* and *thumped*. Its report created a vibration they felt in their chests within the enclosed space as the massive rounds tore through the first three bears. The first creature's ugly face contorted in pain and shock as its body systems shut down due to the hole in its midsection. It toppled aside to reveal the equally ravaged corpses of the other two. Fortunately, the bullets had embedded themselves within the steel of the upward-angled hallway rather than ricocheting off and back.

Others were behind the first three. They piled in too fast for anything like carefully aimed shots.

"God *dammit!*" Dante snarled as he swung his gun's muzzle toward the face of the nearest bear and intercepted one of its paws. Braelin and Neburu moved into battle to his left and right, although he could not see them amid the general chaos. He squeezed his left hand and deployed the long, sharp blade of his razorfist, punching it into the bear's throat and twisting it.

The creature gurgled and spasmed. Its thrashings nearly

pulled the rifle from Dante's grip, and he stumbled sidelong to regain his balance. The wound he'd inflicted was ghastly enough that the yeti-bear was already dying of massive blood loss.

Then another's claws swiped toward Dante's face while he was still off-balance.

Something flashed. Instead of the claws penetrating his armor or the blow's force knocking him into the freezing water, the creature's paw detached from its arm in a spray of blood. Dante dodged from the stump. The blade from Neburu's gauntlet was stained red as the woman stepped around the injured bear to raise her pulsecore and fire at another a few feet away.

The bear nearest Dante was missing a paw and losing copious amounts of blood, but pain and rage drove it on. It lashed out with its other forepaw while bounding forward. Dante ducked low, slashed it along the leg, and rolled aside. The yeti-like monster toppled over the catwalk's edge to crash into the icy water below, where spider-crabs converged on its body.

Meanwhile, Mugoi climbed the metal ladder along the chamber's wall that led up from the network assembly area to the catwalk. He had both pistols out and maintained his hold on them as he used his wrists and the gun butts to hoist himself up. His augmented reflexes and coordination kept him steady as he ascended.

Above him, Braelin aimed his carbine and fired a single round into the head of a yeti-bear emerging from the hall. The creature's skull came apart in a green and red flash as the round detonated and its headless body fell across the path of the next ones in line, momentarily slowing them.

Mugoi looked down. Two huge crabs had climbed on top of the others and used them to reach some lugs and pipes encircling the room. Their arachnoid limbs found enough purchase to vault themselves upward. They would catch him in seconds.

He hung from the ladder with one hand. The other dropped to

aim his pistol while his opposite foot braced against the wall. He squeezed off six rounds in quick succession, targeting each of the crabs. One round missed, but the other five punched small holes in the animals' carapaces, drawing out oozing streamers of grue as the drill rounds scrambled their soft interiors. They convulsed and fell atop the others, knocking three or four of them aside.

Then Mugoi pulled himself onto the catwalk in time for a yeti-bear's opened, drooling jaws to appear in front of his face.

Braelin shouted, "Hold on!"

Something *whacked* and *thudded* wetly, and the bear jerked in place. Its jaws remained agape rather than closing around the cyborg's head. Mugoi rolled aside. Braelin was behind the beast with his tactical tomahawk's blade embedded in the back of its neck. Mugoi moved to the bear's side and fired one pistol round between its ribs, punching a hole clean through that missed his comrades. The animal slumped over, dead.

Braelin retracted the tomahawk. "Yep. Thank me later."

Mugoi's inhumanly beautiful face showed something close to annoyance at first, but his expression softened. He nodded.

Dante and Neburu had killed enough of the yeti-bears to clear a path out, and the handful of others retreated. "Midas, have you downloaded the schematic stuff?"

"Almost sir, about one more minute."

Dante cursed and looked over the railing. The crabs again piled atop one another to reach the parts of the wall that would give them enough purchase to climb to the catwalk.

He aimed his rifle and fired four rounds, avoiding the walls and the network assembly in the center. Instead, he targeted the crabs near the bottom of the arachnoid pyramid. Several of them exploded into gooey chunks, piles collapsed, and sent frustrated crabs back into the churning mass of ice and water.

The apprentices opened up with their firearms, annihilating most of the remaining creatures. Others surged from under the sea, converging on their position to replace them. The yeti-bears would not stay frightened for long.

Midas announced, *"Got it!"*

Dante exhaled in relief. "Come on," he barked. "Klement, you take point. Mugoi, rear."

"Roger." Braelin sighed and rushed to the threshold of the warped doorway. His carbine was back in both hands, and the tomahawk returned to his waist.

Keeping formation, they clambered back through the sagging hallways, this time having to fight uphill. When at last Braelin pounced over the exit's threshold, he immediately found three more yeti-bears working themselves into a frenzy of vengeful hunger.

"Shit on a shingle!" His carbine came up at once. He blasted the first one, ripping its body apart with small plasma detonations, while Neburu similarly bisected the one to the left, and Dante vaporized the head of the one on the right. All three fell dead practically in unison.

As they marched forward, Mugoi stopped and swung his hands up, firing both pistols repeatedly. A yeti-bear on the cabin roof above them writhed in pain as the drill rounds sawed through its organs and limbs, then plummeted toward the rig's main floor area.

Mugoi lunged forward, shoving against his companions from behind. They stumbled forward, and the whole quartet narrowly missed being smashed by the falling hairy carcass.

Dante blinked. "Thanks." Mugoi's ability to perceive subtle hints of danger was uncanny. He lacked the field of experience of the others, yet his augmentations served him well.

The quartet reached the emergency ladder, the same one they'd used to ascend the platform. As they clambered down, Nasreen addressed them through their comms.

"It's me. Midas sent me a message that you successfully

retrieved the objective. I'm coming in. Should be able to pick you up next to the oil rig."

Dante hopped down to the ice. A shudder ripped through his body as he tried not to slip and fall. The others fanned out around him, checking for other yeti-bears or spider-crabs. It seemed they had killed or driven off all the creatures in the vicinity for now.

He touched his helmet as they moved to a more secure spot near a large ice cliff. "Okay, good. We'll await you."

"Hold on," she interjected. "Things are coming across the ice toward you. I can't get a good look at them because of all the crap blowing on the wind, but they look, well, big and elongated. Like long snaky things or columns of moving creatures. I'm not quite sure. Over."

Dante's heart sank. "That doesn't sound good. Are they going to hit our position before or after you do?"

"If you guys move fast, I should be able to pick you up before they're within visual range."

Since they'd all heard her, Dante didn't have to issue further commands. The shuttle's lights were faint but visible through the gloom to the west. They all hustled toward it as dread rose in their guts.

Nasreen piloted the ship closer to them and descended toward a low, flat hillock of piled ice and snow. The thrusters would start to melt it, but not to the point of threatening any breakthrough to the water beneath, particularly since they'd leave directly.

They were halfway up the slope of the hillock when two yeti-bears burst out from behind an ice stalagmite, growling and extending their dagger-like claws.

Dante hissed, "Shit!" and pivoted his gun toward the closest one, squeezing the trigger barely in time. A .50-cal round punched through the beast's stomach and out its spine, dropping it instantly.

The second one cut Neburu and Braelin off from each other, and the latter again almost lost his footing. Neburu hopped back and shot the bear twice, blowing its arm off and putting a gory crater in its chest. As it slumped, it fell directly into Braelin before he could regain his balance.

"Klement!" Neburu futilely extended her hand to catch him. The small man's eyes bulged as he slipped and tumbled over the edge of the hillock, rolling down the snow-dusted slopes to the mass of ice below.

Mugoi said, "Nasreen is right there. It is unfortunate, but the rest of us can—"

"*No*," Dante thundered. "We are *not* leaving anyone behind. Period. Let's get him."

As he dashed back down the slope, looping toward the point where Braelin had rolled to, the "things" Nasreen had mentioned drew closer. Whatever they were, they were a mass of multiple creatures. They didn't look like yeti-bears.

Dante was out in front. He ran to Braelin's side and took the man's arm as the older Plunderer rose. "I'm fine." He gasped. "Sort of."

Neburu and Mugoi looked irritated, but they said nothing.

Nasreen's voice came again. "What happened? Also, those things are right on top of you now. Do you want me to try to scare them off?"

"No," Dante instructed. "They might be humans, in which case they might have anti-air weapons. Hold on a sec while we figure it out."

He looked out across the ice.

At last, the nature of their visitors was clear. Teams of huge wolfish dogs, like Huskies but larger and more vicious-looking, pulled crude sleighs across the frozen sea. Riding in the primitive but effective vehicles suited for the environment were people or beings close enough to make no difference. They had stocky figures, most with long hair and beards, wore furs, and held various weapons.

Dirtwalkers. From what Dante understood, this area was supposed to be free of human habitation. Their information was clearly in need of updating.

All three apprentices raised their weapons, training them on the approaching figures but holding their fire for the time being.

"Wait." Dante spoke sharply enough for them to grasp that it was a command but not with enough force to startle the newcomers.

The Dirtwalkers noticed the guns and grasped that they were weapons. They responded in kind, hoisting aloft harpoons balanced for throwing and crude but functional crossbows. As primitive as their arsenal was, Dante had little doubt they knew how to use what they had, and he and his companions were within effective range. Their armor would probably protect them, but there was still an element of risk involved in any armed conflict.

Things could potentially get ugly.

Dante added in a softer voice, "I can probably talk us out of this if they speak the Dirtwalker Trade Tongue. They might be too isolated to know it. Don't open fire as long as they hold back. If any of them attack us, annihilate them."

He meant every word of it. If peaceful solutions were possible, they were also preferable. Otherwise, they'd have to eliminate the threat at the first sign of danger. On the ravaged planet Earth, far from civilization, Nature and Fate had no mercy or patience for those who hesitated to defend themselves.

Out in front at the center of the convoy of sleighs was a broad-shouldered man with iron-streaked hair, older than the others but still vital and powerful-looking. It was all but certain that he was the chief of their tribe, or at least a trusted captain of this particular war band.

Midas piped up then, speaking directly into the audio processing centers of Dante's brain.

"Sir. I can provide a certain degree of linguistic analysis that you may find useful. We have enough fragments of different strains of the Dirtwalker Trade Tongue, which vary somewhat from region to region as dialects tend to. We also have a longstanding database of the various, mostly Scandinavian languages indigenous to this region. Plus the languages most commonly spoken by immigrant populations in the area at the time of the planet's abandonment. All of which should—"

Dante interrupted him. "Yes. Good. Do that." He kept his volume low, so the Dirtwalkers would not think he was speaking to them, but there was no mistaking his tone. Midas knew not to challenge him when he spoke that way.

"Very well." The AI fell silent.

The sleighs came to a gradual stop. The chief climbed down and stood before them on the ice. He held their gaze while his warriors kept their weapons trained on the outlanders.

Dante realized with growing curiosity and alarm that the people before him were much different than he had expected. Despite their ragged condition and long separation from the people of the Stations, most Dirtwalkers were identifiable as members of *Homo sapiens*.

These Dirtwalkers more resembled pictures of Neanderthals that Dante had seen in holobooks when he was a kid. They were all shorter than typical humans. The tallest appeared to be around five-foot-three-inches and of stocky build with broad, blunt, heavy facial features.

That by itself was enough to pique his curiosity. The hairs on the back of his neck stood straight when he saw that not all of the fur that enswathed them belonged to the dead animal pelts they wore. Some of it was theirs—a thick fuzzy matting that grew on their arms and legs.

The people who had remained on Earth were changing. For this tribe or race, it must have been a series of mutations to help protect them from the cold. Dante could think of no other explanation.

Then the chieftain barked in a low, rumbling voice, "You, strangers! Get away from here. You have desecrated the…" He lapsed into several words that Dante didn't recognize before resuming, "And go this instant! Or you must die." Although recognizable as a subset of the Trade Tongue, the accent and rhythm of his speech were profoundly alien.

To buy them time, Dante held up a hand, empty palm out in the universal human gesture of reconciliation. "We are leaving now. We mean you no harm and do not want to fight."

Midas chimed in. *"There were one or two words I could not translate, probably names. It seems this is a holy site and they expect anyone who comes here to pay tribute. I believe he wants something of the sort from you before you can leave."*

Dante's spirits sank into his gut, which felt like it was descending in an elevator. Unless he could figure out how to placate the chief, they might have to kill all of the poor bastards and risk injury or death in the process.

His apprentices' gazes flicked toward him. They were getting antsy. Everyone was waiting.

Dante inhaled. "We did not know of your customs. We wish only to leave in peace. If you would ask an offering, what do you want from us?"

If they wanted the life of one of their number, all negotiations were over. If they wanted food, a trinket, or perhaps a weapon, he would be willing to talk it over.

The chief's face stretched out in disbelief at Dante's ignorance and foolishness. "Only something of great value can account for this disgrace!" His voice echoed across the polar wastes, deflected by the nearby ice cliff.

"You have come here as thieves and trespassers, have you not? We shall have your treasure, then. Your mightiest weapon, or whatever we may trade for the most food."

Mugoi spoke in a soft voice colder than the wind around them. "We are *not* giving them the spoils of the mission, sir. Are we?"

Dante made up his mind at once. A mighty weapon was a reasonable price to pay.

"So be it," he told the tribal leader. He ejected the empty magazine from his rifle and slapped in a fresh one. "My weapon shall be your tribute. It is very dangerous but will serve you well. I can show you how to use it if you pledge not to use it against *us* and allow us to leave with our lives."

The older man's eyes glimmered with growing excitement. "Yes, that is good. Give it here!"

There was a chance the chief would accidentally shoot them, his companions, or himself, but it was likely preferable to an all-out fight between the two groups. Dante walked toward the chief, holding the gun away from his body with the muzzle aimed at the ground, and handed it to him butt-first.

The chieftain snatched it with thick-fingered hands and held it, marveling at its gleaming surface, strange contours, and incomprehensible parts. He did not seem to grasp the weapon's most fundamental nature since he put one hand on the barrel and another halfway up the chassis as if he were holding a club and assumed the stock was the business end.

Dante was about to give him a basic lesson in gun safety when a guttural howl sounded above them, and a big, furry white shape fell into their midst from the cliffs.

Neburu shouted, "Dante! Get back!" He was in her line of fire.

Dante sprang aside and backed up while drawing his knife, cursing himself for giving away the gun before he'd explained how to use it. He sensed his other apprentices fanning out to get a clear shot at the yeti-bear.

Then a brownish shape streaked through the air. A more or less human voice snarled in rage, and the white body toppled over. Dante watched in shock as the chieftain swung the gun again and again into the creature's head, caving in its skull and reducing most of it to a pulpy mess. The monster groaned and fell still, aside from its limbs spasming.

The old chief looked up at them, laughing and twirling the heavy rifle around in his hands as if it weighed no more than a thin stick. Although short, his people seemed to possess immense strength.

"Yes, yes! This is a good weapon. You have our thanks. Go now in peace." He waved them off while his warriors cackled and cheered. A couple dismounted to secure the yeti-bear's corpse. They would probably have it for dinner.

Dante nodded. "Yes. Thank you, and farewell." He turned his head to his companions, arched his eyebrows, and inclined his head toward their ship.

Klement coughed. "Don't have to say a word, boss. We're all on our way."

Camaraderie and relief spread through them as they jogged across the ice and up the slope to the hovering shuttle. They'd accomplished their mission together and came out all in one piece at the end. Mugoi seemed disappointed that things with the Dirtwalkers had gone so peacefully.

CHAPTER THREE

They had more than enough money to replace the rifle. Dante knew that. Still, it irked him. He didn't like unnecessary losses of equipment or the extra expenditures it took to deal with them. Or the inefficiency and irresponsibility of it. Meanwhile, there was no shortage of other weaponry on the shuttle, plus their entire arsenal back at headquarters.

Nasreen broke the silence that had settled over the crew as they came out of the turbulence of Earth's atmosphere and into the brief stretch of open space before they returned to the Stations.

"I have to admit, it's nice to always head back to the same place. Jumping around from Station to Station and trying to remember where all my safehouses were was kind of a pain in the ass. Right, Dante?"

She caught his eyes via the mirror above the cockpit. It looked out of place in a shuttle but served as a non-tech backup in case someone took out the camera feeds in the rear bay.

He nodded. "Yeah. You did what you had to do since lying low and being as concealed as possible was how to play the game. Now, of course, everyone knows who we are anyway."

She chuckled. "Or at least, they used to. I keep forgetting how quickly people forget about celebrities as soon as they—we—are no longer in the public eye."

She was right. A year ago, E-zex and the Hellcat had been household names, among the most famous people in the known world. They had streamed their exploits as Plunderers, bringing the exciting and dangerous activities of those who went Dirtside into the living rooms of millions. In doing so, they had also toppled Slaine Solar Solutions, one of the most powerful companies in orbital civilization.

Everyone still knew who they were. Dante had shed his former alias of Jordan Raksha, but the moniker "Hellcat" had stuck with him. People greeted Nasreen as "E-zex" far more often than "Ms. Joelle." Granted, she'd been a former freelance espionage agent, accustomed to keeping a low profile and rotating between multiple false identities.

Braelin stretched, and something *popped*. "Ugh, the elbow always does that," he complained. "Eh, whatever. We've got rice beer left in the fridge, right? I forgot to check before we left."

Midas spoke aloud for the first time since the start of the mission. "Yes, Mr. Klement. You asked me to keep track of that three days ago, and I made a note of it."

Dante shuddered as the artificial voice receded. Hearing a computer speak through his head was still unnerving. He preferred that Midas not do it unless necessary. Originally it had been worse. The vibrations made him feel like someone was sticking something into his ear. Since then, they'd upgraded his voice module to something smoother and more sophisticated, but he still disliked it.

Braelin grinned. "Good man, Midas. Good man."

Normally not one to crack jokes, Neburu pointed out, "I believe Dante is the man of the hour. But yes, I think I will have a beer as well. We have more than earned it." Despite all they'd been through, she had somehow retained the ladylike mystique that always surrounded her. She might as well have stepped out of a fashion ad. How she did it was some form of female magic beyond Dante's understanding.

Mugoi had kept silent until now. "The knowledge of our success is itself the greatest reward. That reminds me, Captain. How would you grade our performance?" The insinuation in his soft voice was obvious.

Dante coughed. "You all pass. Congratulations. As for the specifics, let's deal with that later after we have time to recuperate. Again, I expect you all to be aware when you make mistakes and to continue learning from them."

Braelin and Neburu turned to one another and high-fived, an unexpected but appropriate gesture of victory. Mugoi was more subdued, but his strange face relaxed into a smile, and he nodded.

Nasreen added, "Yeah, congrats. We're almost home." The Atlantica docks attached to the vast domed structure loomed ahead.

Atlantica Central Station was the unofficial capital of the entire orbital human civilization. Technically, each Station was a city-state with its own rules, laws, and customs, but all were linked. A net-like latticework of tubes and tunnels connected them in an irregular ring surrounding Earth.

Atlantica Metro had not been the largest city on the mother planet, but it had nonetheless been massive. It was a major center of political negotiation, business intrigue, and technological innovation. Experiments long ago with Atlanticore crystal and its resonance properties were part of what had enabled Earth's major cities to rise to the stars after merely shielding them from the increasingly hostile elements had proved insufficient.

Like most of the Stations, it was also located more or less directly above its original location. In this case, the North

Atlantic off the northeastern coast. That made it convenient to reach the Stations corresponding to any cities in the Americas, Europe, or Africa. It had connection tubes to more fellow Stations than any other in the new space-bound world.

Nasreen had chosen it as the logical location for their crew's permanent HQ. Dante had not objected. He found the city agreeable enough in addition to its prestige and convenience.

They landed at the docks, which were busy as usual. Gliding into a long bay behind a line of other ships, mostly commuters between Stations, they joined the queue for the harbormaster's inspection.

Their shuttle was a model cleared for intra-city travel, which meant they only had to log their arrival information and be released into the streets rather than dock and take public transport home. Nobody unbuckled from their seats.

With the mundane paperwork done, the gates into the Station proper opened. Nasreen piloted them onto the main encircling highway around the equator of Atlantica Metro before getting into a sky lane and taking the shortest route to the district where they were based. It didn't take long. Traffic was substantial but flowed smoothly. Atlantica's drivers tended to be less obnoxious than some other cities.

Their neighborhood was a middle-class, business-oriented one closer to the center of town than Dante would have preferred. It meant a longer trip out to the rim whenever they needed to go Dirtside, but it was acceptable. It kept them within range of most of the places they needed or wanted to go in town.

As they approached, Dante's thoughts returned to everything they had done on the mission. "You three," he addressed the apprentices. "Like I said, you all passed, but none of you passed with flying colors. There's room for improvement with each of you.

"Watching your footing and always keeping your balance. Watching your ammo count and managing your reloads. Conferring with other team members before taking drastic actions. Those are three things you need to work on.

"The whole operation could have been faster. Had we made it back to the shuttle even one minute sooner, I wouldn't have had to give away an expensive rifle."

Their sinking spirits were tangible, but they needed to hear it. Giving out praise too freely and withholding legitimate criticism was a recipe for sloppiness and overconfidence. Still, they'd all done *well enough*—for now.

Nasreen brought the shuttle out of the sky lane and put it in hover as they merged onto a ground-level street. From there, it was only another minute or two back to HQ.

The building they had selected was originally an office they converted into an all-purpose Marauder facility. It had sleeping quarters for all five of them, an armory, infirmary, a kitchen and dining area, storage space, a room for martial arts training, and a multipurpose recreation and meeting chamber. Pretty much everything they needed under one roof.

Nasreen opened their garage and guided the shuttle in. A standard-sized hovercar occupied the remaining space. The shuttle took up more room than a strictly Station-bound craft.

As she powered the ship down, Dante announced, "Everyone stow your gear, get cleaned up and grab a refreshment, but nothing that will weigh you down or take too long. We're debriefing in the rec room before I cut anyone loose."

Braelin half-sighed, half-groaned. "Fine, I guess."

"You don't have to guess because that's an order," Dante retorted. "You have twenty-five minutes. Get to it." He didn't want to coddle them. They needed to understand that working for him meant *business*.

Still, their high spirits after the initial success had all but crashed and burned, and the exertion and stress of the mission had taken their toll. They all seemed tired and mopey as they gathered their things and hustled out of the ship. They headed for the armory and storage first, then presumably to their private quarters for a few minutes of peace.

Dante and Nasreen secured the shuttle and walked side by side to the rec room. The place was still rather sparsely furnished. Nasreen wanted more decoration to make them feel at home or impress guests if they should ever have them. Dante gave little thought to such things and was more concerned with the place's structural integrity, defensibility, and keeping its emergency stores well-stocked. Aside from such practical matters, it already had all the essential comforts. Beds. Chairs. Coffee makers. Stuff like that.

Dante was making coffee when Nasreen spoke, and he knew there was nothing he could do. There would be no escape. They were about to have an argument.

She crossed her arms. "Dante, why did you yell at them as we got closer to home? Braelin falling off the slope toward the end was something that should have been avoided, yes. Otherwise, they did well.

"We achieved the objective and got out with all of us in one piece, which is nothing to despise given how dangerous the conditions were. They deserve encouragement. You could always remind them of minor stuff that needs improvement after they've had time to relax and celebrate."

He exhaled. "If I do that, they'll pass out right afterward and forget half of what I said. By reminding them of it now, they'll think it over *while* they're relaxing. Makes it easier to remember it all."

She snapped, "If they underestimate their abilities, or if they get too concerned about never being good enough to meet your standards, they won't grow into their roles and be able to trust themselves."

She went on in that vein for several minutes. Dante interrupted her with anecdotes of how he'd trained other people in the past using the same methods and had always ended up with good results. He politely refrained from bringing up the time he'd spent training *her*.

Midway into their debate, someone knocked on the door. Nasreen was still railing about "group cohesion" as she went to wave off the apprentices, indicating they should wait there or go elsewhere until she and Dante finished talking.

He rebuffed her, pointing out that they intended to offload some of their responsibilities onto the trio soon and how letting them know everything they needed to work on would bring that about sooner.

Then, to their surprise, Midas offered his two cents, speaking aloud.

"Oh, that reminds me," the AI's voice rang out. "As you asked, I performed a search on the Chorus and may have a lead that we could pursue if you still wish to do so. How would that affect our current timeline?"

Dante suddenly wanted to reach into his brain and pull the AI out. It was rare for Midas to annoy him to this extent. His usually silent companion should have known better than to blab about that right in front of Nasreen.

Nasreen's eyes bulged. "What? I thought we agreed to stop wasting our time worrying about that!"

"No," Dante grumbled. "You kept saying that over and over again. I never agreed to anything. I waited for you to run out of steam."

Her pitch and volume rose. "Why are you so obsessed with that? Yes, it was weird and disturbing, but it was a one-time instance. We have other things to concern ourselves with."

When they confronted Cormac Slaine in his hidden bunker, a multitude of disembodied voices had hijacked Midas and broadcast a mixture of threats, warnings, and cryptic statements through him. Dante had pretended to forget about it at first. He could not.

"No guarantee it will remain one-time." His eyes narrowed as he poured himself a cup of coffee.

It was the memory of the way the Chorus had *controlled* him. The humiliation of being rendered all but helpless by a foe who refused to show their faces or disclose their nature or location. They were a threatening force that operated purely by misdirection yet had the power to seize hold of someone as blunt and implacable as himself. He could neither forget nor forgive.

Nasreen swiped her hand in front of her chest in a cutting motion.

"No. We should leave well enough alone. The voices haven't come back, have they? It's been a goddamn year.

"The only place we encountered them was in a high-tech facility operated by SSS. It could well have been part of the place's defenses, something they would never be able to replicate elsewhere. Chasing it could create unnecessary problems. We have enough on our plate as it is."

Dante's jaw clenched, and he ground his teeth. He understood. She had a point. Still, he could not get over it and move on. She was a spy by profession. Someone whose task was to blend in and seek efficiency by taking the path of least resistance. A good spy was efficient when they slipped in and out, making as little mess as possible.

Dante was in the business of getting in and out quickly too, but he was a fighter and a hunter—a Marauder. His version of efficiency involved identifying the target and destroying it. Leaving an enemy drifting in the breeze with no idea of when they might strike next for a *year* was not his idea of wisdom.

By now he'd learned that it was useless to try to sway her by simply repeating himself emphatically or using a stern tone. It only annoyed her and inspired her to work around him through indirect means. He needed to *convince* her. Of course, if she refused to be convinced, remaining stalwart was still his Plan B.

"We have apprentices," he pointed out. "Taking them on and

training them was mostly your idea, as you may recall. You felt that we needed to pass on our knowledge and experiences—to compensate for losing some fame since we stopped streaming. Also because it's a tough job and having more than two people doing it helps. Right?"

She pursed her lips and stared into his eyes. She was probably trying to figure out his angle so she could head off whatever argument he was about to make. "Yes. That much is true. You were and probably still are the greatest Plunderer ever to go Dirtside, and I mean, I'm not half-bad either. We should leave behind a legacy, and having disciples is a good way to go about that. Which is why—"

"Which is *exactly* why we need to protect them. If those voices come back at an inopportune time, it could endanger them. Or I could be endangered and die before I finish teaching them everything I know. Pretty damn inconvenient.

"Plus, having them around to handle some of the grunt work frees up some of *our* time. Or mine, at least. We could afford for me to slip off and snoop around while you continue their education or look for the next job."

Her mouth dropped open. "What happens if you finally stumble into the job you can't handle by yourself? *That* is a better way to get yourself killed prematurely than anything to do with random voices.

"Not to mention, it's not as though no one knows who you are now or about us. If you anger the wrong people, they'll work their way back to HQ or my safehouses. To our apprentices. To me."

He scowled at the wall. "You have a point, but not a good enough one for me to give up. I need to know what caused the Chorus, who's behind it, and whether I still have to worry about them.

"I don't want anything bad to happen to you. Any of you. But you will not convince me to back off on this. I'm doing it, no matter what."

She stared at him. Her eyes bulged, and her lip trembled before she abruptly threw up her hands and spun. "Ohh, goddammit. God *dammit*, Dante! You stubborn, abrasive, pompous asshole! Do you know what your problem is?"

"That I'm stubborn, abrasive, and pompous? Just a guess."

"That." She pointed at him and raised her voice. "But not only that. You go out of your way to butt heads against people.

"It's like you deliberately take minor shit and treat it like it's far worse and more important than it is because it gives you an excuse to 'stand your ground' and be at odds with me or whoever else is disagreeing with you. You're a mindless, reflexive contrarian. If I told you not to jump off a one-hundred-story building, you would immediately look for excuses to do exactly that."

Dante had no idea where she got such a notion from. "No, I'm not. If you're going to make up fictitious examples, maybe I should start doing shit like that to make you feel like you can predict the future."

Nasreen choked, and for a second he thought she was about to choke *him* as her hands clawed toward his neck. Then she let out another ragged "Ohhh," stomped away from him, yanked open the door, and vanished down the hall. The door slammed behind her, and the footsteps receded.

Dante stood alone in the big, empty meeting room, slowly chewing on his thoughts.

"Midas," he muttered after a minute or so. "Why the hell did you say the search results out loud? There was no reason for Nasreen to hear them."

He wasn't sure he wanted an answer. Getting the wrong one might make him suddenly interested in removing the AI implant from his skull.

"Well, I must admit, I felt it was appropriate for everyone to be aware. I do not like the notion of us hiding things from Nasreen. If we are going to have any success locating the Voices, the Chorus, or what-

ever you call it, it's best to handle it as a team. That is what has allowed us to be so successful up to this point."

Dante's jaw muscles tightened again. "Oh."

The AI hurried on as though he had something to say before Dante blew up at him. *"Also, the results I've found so far suggest the Voices were using a primary communication relay to transmit down to the surface. If you'd like, we could poke around the relay in question to see if there's any evidence of tampering."*

His anger faded. Curiosity and excitement rose to replace it. He rubbed his stubbled chin. "That's interesting. Yeah. Give me a second here to process that."

Telling Nasreen about it might—*might*—convince her to come to her senses and help him, or at least give him her moral support for what he planned to do.

Then again, it could spark another ugly, stupid, counterproductive fight over basically nothing. He had no desire to deal with anything of that nature.

"Nah," he mumbled. "Seems like she needs to go blow off some steam, anyway. It's the perfect opportunity for us to get going." He ought to rest after all they'd dealt with on the North Sea earlier. Still, it was better to take golden opportunities than waste them.

"You mean tonight?"

"Yeah." He stretched. "Right after a shower and a cup of coffee."

CHAPTER FOUR

Nasreen pulled open the door and stormed out. The three apprentices had already departed by the time she left Dante behind. Slamming the door, she headed straight for the kitchen, which struck her as the place they were most likely to be.

"No. Wait." She stopped in the hallway, out of sight and earshot from anyone, and looked at the floor while she breathed in and out, gradually wiping away her anger, extinguishing the flames of it, but allowing the coals to keep smoldering.

When she was this aggravated, there was usually a good reason for it, so she tried not to forget why it had happened. Later, when calmer, it would be easier to deal with.

She stood straight again. "Okay, then. No reason to let this ruin our evening. We succeeded." She nodded and continued the rest of the way down the hall to the doorway that led to the kitchen and dining area.

Braelin, Neburu, and Mugoi had all gathered, helping themselves to a bottle of beer each while they attempted to scrabble together something approximating dinner. Braelin was handling most of the food and chatting up Neburu, who languished in a chair nearby. Mugoi leaned against the wall, watching and listening but not participating much in the conversation.

Although they were trying to wind down and did not seem *unhappy,* there was an underlying sulkiness. It wasn't only because of Dante's uncalled-for criticisms of their performance at the last minute. It was also because they could tell that he and Nasreen had been fighting *again* and it probably meant the tensions would linger throughout the building for at least another day or two.

Mugoi noticed her at once. "Welcome. Hope you and Dante had a nice chat."

"Ha, ha. That's one way of putting it. He's being stubborn and tactless as usual. He does have your three's best interests in mind, but he's terrible at expressing it in ways that are... I don't know. Constructive? Pleasant? He has no people skills to speak of. He invested all of his abilities in *other* skills."

Neburu quipped, "Yes, we had noticed. It is an honor to learn from him, although some honors are more fun than others."

The implications of what she'd said—specifically, what she *hadn't* said—were not lost on Nasreen. "Exactly. I keep trying to convince him that it doesn't cost him anything to make it a little more fun."

Braelin shrugged. He had taken a skillet down, placed it on the stove, and was pulling egg mix and vegetables from the cooling unit. "Well, he probably needs a decent meal, same as us. I was going to make omelets if that's okay. We're out of cheese, but we got the egg and veg. It's a start."

Nasreen tapped her lips. "I have some quick rice as well. We could make fried rice instead. It might be more filling and would better maximize the use of our ingredients. Ugh, I'm talking like *him* now, aren't I?"

"Perhaps," Mugoi purred. "Perhaps a little. You two are not all that different."

She turned and glared at him. "Only in that we're the two best

Marauders in the business. Otherwise, we differ quite a bit, *thank you.*"

Mugoi shrugged. Like all his—its—movements, it was so perfectly smooth it was uncanny. Nasreen was growing more used to it, but it was impossible to mistake Mugoi for simply a normal human being who looked different. Whether in appearance or personality.

Nasreen pushed past Braelin and found the rice in the cooler, along with another beer for herself. She needed a drink. In fact, several drinks would be better, regardless of what Dante might say about it. An idea occurred to her.

They needed to get out. The whole crew needed to go someplace other than headquarters and for purposes other than business. They needed a night on the town. It would soothe the stupid tensions that were blossoming among them, and they deserved it for a job well done.

She wouldn't invite Dante. Not necessarily out of spite. He would have probably refused. While he didn't mind a nice meal and drink now and then, his lack of social skills made him feel out of place in the more raucous venues.

As the apprentices took to joking, arguing, and venting mainly between Braelin and Neburu with occasional comments from Mugoi, Nasreen decided against broaching the idea right now. First, food.

Neburu asked, "Do we have any side dishes to go with this?" She chopped vegetables and threw them into the pan alongside the rice. They held back on the eggs for now.

Braelin offered, "Isn't there some chicken salad or something in the back of the cooler? Hell, I'm not picky."

There was, and while Nasreen had never specifically heard of anyone pairing the two, she couldn't complain.

Everyone except Mugoi contributed to the overall process of completing their dinner. After meeting Dante, Nasreen had to admit—to herself, if not out loud—that he was the better cook between them. In the time they had known each other she'd picked up a few things from his store of knowledge and tricks. By the time the fried rice was ready, it smelled wonderful, tasted nearly as good, and wasn't too bad on texture.

Everyone sat to eat, adding a dollop of the chicken salad to the spare room on their plates and washing it down with what remained of their beers or simply with water.

Braelin took a huge mouthful. "Not bad, not bad. We need to do this more often, instead of throwing money away on takeout or eating packaged shit. I mean yeah, you can't do much cooking when you're on the shuttle, let alone Dirtside, but when we're home. Good teamwork exercise, plus the food is better."

"Indeed," Neburu agreed with a pleasant air of serenity. "There is something primal in human beings preparing meals together and eating together in this fashion. Nature intended us to do it from our earliest days."

Nasreen nodded. "It's something that *doesn't* separate us from the Dirtwalkers, that is for certain. A lot of them are dangerous, but Dante and I have had plenty of experience with ones who aren't so bad if you approach them right."

Mugoi was eating with light but steady forkfuls. He chuckled. "I may not be strictly *human* anymore, but perhaps you are correct. The old rituals still have some symbolic value."

It was the type of comment Nasreen had grown to expect from him, a curious mixture of elitism with legitimate intellectual curiosity. He, it, or whatever he was, would never be an easy person to grow close to, yet his role among them was becoming more and more defined as time went on. Despite his overcompetitiveness, he usually did a damn good job.

Midway into supper, Nasreen decided the time was right. The subject that most needed broaching was one that the other three would never raise on their own. They didn't think it was "their place" to speak up.

"Well," she began and sighed heavily with exasperation. "Dante is being his old self again. I was his apprentice about a year and a half ago, you know. I think he's snappier with you three because he's training all of you at once, whereas with me there wasn't anyone else. He's still the same Dante. He means well, but his communication skills, empathy, and patience could stand some improvement."

As she'd expected, the newer crew members looked surprised that she would say such a thing in front of them. Then the surprise transformed into agreement—and annoyance that she was correct.

Braelin grunted. "He's a hard man to work for. Fair, and he knows his stuff, but it isn't easy, is it?"

Neburu set her fork down and folded her hands. "Yes. He gives broad praise, saying 'well done' here and there, but is far more specific in his criticism. It would be helpful if his praise was equally specific. We never know quite what we are doing *right*, only what we are doing wrong."

Mugoi added, "Perhaps he ought to assign a score to our actions and performance. That would make it clearer who is doing best and where the improvement is most required."

Nodding, Nasreen guided them through a brief discussion while they finished their meal. Later she could present Dante with a summary of all they'd talked about. It might not get through their leader's hardened skull and stubborn personality, but he was more apt to listen to Nasreen than anyone else.

Setting down her fork, she announced, "I imagine we all needed to get that out of our system. Now that we've had a nice meal, I think what we need next is a night on the town. I'm serious." She clapped once. "Everyone get ready. We're going out for a drink."

Neburu arched her eyebrows and Mugoi stared at her blankly, but Klement had the most obvious reaction.

"Shit. I mean, I'm pretty tired, but then again I might be

getting my second wind. That does sound pretty damn good right about now. Ladies and Mugoi, what do you say?"

Neburu rolled her shoulders. "Sure, I suppose."

Mugoi ran a sleek finger along his perfectly symmetrical chin. "I am unaccustomed to dressing for venues of this sort. My usual tactical gear would not be appropriate."

"True." Nasreen stood. "We'll help you find something better. There's a decent variety in wardrobe around this place nowadays. You don't have to dress *too* impressively. Simply looking snappy casual ought to be enough."

Braelin grumbled, "It's the snappy part I have trouble with. Not so much the casual."

Twenty minutes later, all four stood in the back storage quarters that doubled as a wardrobe and changing room, typically for when they needed to put on their gear and armor for a mission. It held a full complement of battle paraphernalia for no bullshit Dirtside runs and the more subtle sorts of armor and less obtrusive weapons and tools for jobs in the Stations that required greater finesse.

The latter type of job—Nasreen's specialty before she had met Dante—had led them to accumulate a decent selection of different kinds of clothes. One needed to blend into one's environment, whatever that environment might be. Since becoming a high-profile outfit, others sometimes called upon them to attend everything from formal corporate meetings to luxury galas and conferences of roughneck Plunderers and mercenaries. Variety was paramount.

Nasreen focused on helping Mugoi while Braelin and Neburu helped each other.

"Okay," Nasreen began. "First of all, we can lose the holsters and webbing. That is a good general Station rule for anywhere not typically frequented by Plunderers. Didn't we have this discussion before?"

Mugoi smirked. "We may have. I believe in being prepared,

however. My credentials as your and Dante's trainee are easy enough to produce in case law enforcement grows curious."

Nasreen crossed her arms and shook her head. Mugoi was technically correct and as usual, enjoyed flouting social convention wherever and whenever possible. He, or it, also took great pleasure in emphasizing its status as a person who existed outside the usual legal constraints.

The Stations were fragile environments. The great domes that surrounded them, providing gravity and atmosphere, had been constructed to be as hardy as possible. They were also incredibly complex machines that required frequent maintenance and needed all parts working together correctly.

Each city-state prohibited guns, explosives, and plasma weapons due to the extreme danger posed by the threat of depressurization, the failure of atmosphere and gravity generators, or numerous other catastrophic technical difficulties. Orbit-bound humanity had regressed to using melee-range bladed weapons, truncheons, and personal electrical devices, along with the occasional dart launcher or crossbow.

Dirtside, things were an entirely different story. The Earth was already in bad enough shape that a few fiery battles with military-grade weapons technology between rival Plunderers or Plunderers and Dirtwalkers would not make much of a difference. Except to those reduced to carbon particles in the carnage.

Nasreen responded, "You may have all your certification, but it's still best to avoid scaring people unnecessarily. Besides, it's distasteful. People will think you're bragging about your status as a Marauder and fishing for questions about it. Which might impress a few college girls but will come across as tacky to most everyone else."

Mugoi considered it, again stroking his chin with a long, sleek finger. "I suppose it is better to approach such matters with an appreciation for class. What might you recommend I wear instead?"

Nasreen scanned the wardrobe. "I have a suit that will probably fit you." She was relatively tall for a woman, with a significant amount of lean muscle. Mugoi had a similar frame, and at worst her clothes might be a tad snug. "It's a nice one, but not excessively formal or ostentatious. You already attract attention on your own, so you don't need to wear anything flashy."

"True." Mugoi looked well-pleased with the compliments. Nasreen took note. The downside of his aloofness and competitiveness was that he was susceptible to flattery.

Meanwhile, Neburu was holding up and examining a sleek burgundy dress, trying to determine how much skin it would show. It looked like it would probably be exactly the right amount—baring her shoulders and lower legs, enough to catch an eye or two, but still quite tasteful. They had bought it specifically for her a couple of months ago, but she had yet to try it on.

Braelin watched her. "That color suits you. The cut looks right too, if I may say so."

She smiled gently. "You may. Are you planning to wear that leather jacket I saw you in last month? It suited you well. It was the sort of thing that would be equally welcome in a club as it was at the arms sale."

He chuckled. "I suppose it would. I'm too damn short to look like a badass without the right sort of accessories. Of course, there's always my grizzled handsomeness."

"Perhaps." Neburu enjoyed giving the vaguest, most ambiguous answer she could come up with.

Soon, everyone was ready. Nasreen walked with the rest of them to the lobby. They would be departing on foot and had no need for their shuttle. Then she deviated into the hall she had left behind not long before.

She called toward the meeting room, "Hey, Dante. We're going out for a drink."

After a second's delay, his gruff response floated back. "Only one?"

"Yes. The plan is to purchase a single beer and split it among us. Drink, singular." She wondered if he would get the joke, given how literal-minded he could be. "I'd ask if you want to come, but that would probably be pointless if I'm not mistaken." She didn't bother masking her tone's slightly bitter and critical edge.

He might have laughed softly at that, but she couldn't hear if so. "Yeah. I've got other stuff I want to do. Have fun and be smart."

"Bye." She turned and walked back down the hall, rejoining the apprentices in the lobby. "Okay, let's go. We don't have to be out long. I know we're all tired. Trust me, as someone who's been in the business for years—we need this."

They all nodded. She had forgotten, momentarily, that none of them were *complete* rookies. The trio had already been accumulating minor successes as independent Plunderers of various sorts when they'd applied to work with her and Dante. They were up-and-comers, people with enough experience in the sort of work they did that they could become truly great with the help of quality mentors.

Braelin Klement had been a Harvester and Marauder. He had a broad but shallow range of experience collecting and retrieving things from dangerous locales. Neburu had specialized in Marauding, which was the focus of Dante's and Nasreen's operations—acquiring high-value objects or substances from potentially hostile locations.

Mugoi had also done some Marauder work but was primarily a Reaper, which would not have surprised Nasreen if she were to meet him for the first time all over again. Reapers were combatants. Their focus was attacking either rival Plunderer teams or tribes of Dirtwalkers and gathering up the spoils of battle. Dante had worked as a Reaper during his Jordan Raksha phase and had proved quite talented. Combat was considered secondary to Marauding, but Mr. Shale had seen plenty of it.

Then again, so had Nasreen. She had no doubt it was a trend

that would continue. Earth was a dangerous place, and the Stations were sometimes little better.

Outside, the Station was dim with artificial twilight. The city's nightlife scene was stirring from its daytime torpor. Things would get interesting soon.

They had decided on a bar only seven blocks from their headquarters. Nasreen had been there once before with a client during the slow hours, but her impression was that the place grew far more interesting at its peak. Its overall character was appropriate to the level of dress they'd selected—moderately upscale but not fancy enough to intimidate those who were unused to top-end places.

The town bustled around them. Atlantica Metro had been an ostentatious and important city from the earliest days of its inception long ago, and surprisingly little had changed in that regard since most of the city had been lifted out of the earth and relocated to space. The crowds were a mixed and motley bunch even by the standards of huge metropolises. Atlantica had been a destination for the world's flotsam plus its best, brightest, and most ambitious for many decades.

The club was known as the Orchard, and out front was a pair of towering apple tree holograms, luminous in the relative darkness of the artificial evening. The people drifting in had dressed to the same level of swank as the quartet. Some of them eyed the four as they approached. Mugoi drew a lot of glances both hesitant and appreciative. Cyborgs usually did.

When they came to the front doors, the bouncers looked them over for a second, lingering in particular on Mugoi, then shrugged and waved them in. Nasreen smiled at them, hoping to convey that they had made the right choice. If they'd tried to deny them entrance, she might have had to pull the "Do you know who I am?" routine and force her way in through sheer power of clout.

Indoors the place was dim but not exactly dark, with lots of faux-neon and holograms in place of physical decorations. The architecture was sparse to allow more room for the dance floor. Music burbled in the background, loud enough to dance to but not enough to interrupt the conversations of the people hanging out and drinking.

The four went up to the bar and ordered a round of martinis. They all fancied something more upscale after the nice-but-basic rice beer they'd had at home.

The bartender who slid Nasreen's drink to her gave her a sidelong, narrow-eyed glance that at first aroused her suspicions of danger, but the way he shrugged it off let her relax again. He probably was trying to figure out if she was a certain celebrity.

Braelin looked around with a critical eye before nodding in satisfaction. "Nice place. Seems like the crowd's a little young for me, but I mean, look at this jacket. *Always* in style."

Neburu conceded, "It is a nice jacket. Besides, the lighting is too dim to get a good look at anyone's face unless you are right next to a light or hologram."

Mugoi tittered. "I do not seem to have such problems." As usual, he never missed an opportunity to one-up his fellows.

A man wandered up to Nasreen. "Hey there. This your first time here?"

She regarded him coolly. He wasn't bad looking but was pretty drunk and seemed a tad oafish. "No." She took a sip. "I've been here, oh, twice before, although the crowd changes every time."

"Ohh. Ha," he chortled, thinking she'd made a joke, which she hadn't. "Yeah, lot of turnover. It's a popular place, though. Heard some famous people came in who..."

Then the fog of inebriation cleared from his brain as his eyes lit up. "Wait. Aren't you E-zex? The lady who worked with Dante Shale? Holy shit!"

Nasreen smiled a nice, diplomatic smile, although she didn't much feel like it internally. She did not want to think about

Dante right now. It was irritating that she was less famous for her exploits than for being Dante's associate.

"Yes," she confirmed. Around them, other people's conversations faded as more faces turned their way. The mere mention of her business partner's name had captured people's attention more than anything else they'd heard that evening.

A college-aged girl sidled up. "Wow, really? You worked with the Hellcat? Oh, wait, I saw you on there too! You guys were amazing together. Why don't you stream anymore?"

That made Nasreen feel a little better, and her smile grew in size and sincerity.

She waved it off while sipping her drink. "We had other priorities and accomplished most of what we set out to do at the time. Sometimes I miss it. Perhaps we'll start up again. It seems like we still have fans, after all."

There had been rumors that they were a flash in the pan, a trend that faded when they vanished from the public eye. Instead, people remembered them. They'd made an impression.

The apprentices took note and butted in, each of them describing things they'd done, mainly things they'd done alongside Dante or that he had praised them for, to the increasingly rapt and adoring crowd. The onlookers gasped or laughed as Braelin, Neburu, and Mugoi took turns. Nasreen held back, offering short quips or clarifications. She didn't want to hog the spotlight.

She wasn't really in the mood. They had come here specifically to get away from the man, but his disembodied presence now dominated everything.

Someone offered to buy them a round of drinks. Once the glasses crossed the bar, another guy proposed a toast. "To the Hellcat!"

"*To the Hellcat!*"

It sounded like the entire club had joined in. Dozens of drinks rose, *clinked* against each other, and descended again as everyone downed their booze.

Laughter broke out, and the crowd erupted into dancing and singing as the music swelled. The people running the club had ascertained the mood and wanted to sweep everyone along, having as good and memorable a time as possible. It made for repeat customers.

Nasreen tried not to think too hard and allowed the enthusiasm and good cheer to take her. She swayed with the music, enjoying the faint buzz of tipsiness, danced with a few random men who eyed her appreciatively, and debated whether or not to go home with at least one of them. After three songs, there was a break in the soundtrack and most of the dancers returned to the bar.

"You know," Braelin observed, in a voice that was starting to slur, "it's, um, kind of ironic that Dante is the whole reason we had to get out and party to begin with, and now it's, you know, because of his name that we're having such a good time. Hah!" He downed the last of his drink and looked around for another.

Nasreen smirked. It was good to know he was on the same page as she, even if it took the aging cowboy a little longer to reach the same conclusions.

Neburu kept an eye on him. "That is true, and the irony has not been lost on me. Furthermore, the next one should probably be your final drink. We don't want to have *too* much fun."

He scowled but acquiesced. "True enough." When the next glass appeared in front of him on the bar, he looked at it critically and sipped it with a noticeable degree of restraint.

Then Mugoi, whose judgment was perhaps a little impaired, decided to perform a stunt.

Nasreen snapped to attention, her mind and body instantly shifting into what she thought of as "serious mode." The poise and level of alertness necessarily accompanied any change of situation that could become dangerous.

Next to her, Mugoi stood straight and jumped. He vaulted above the heads of the various milling patrons, caught a lower-hanging bar attached to the ceiling, and swung around it in a circle like a gymnast. Then he flipped up in an arc and cannon-balled straight toward another parallel bar.

The club's dim lights reflected off the cyborg's smooth skin as he rotated through the air with his limbs tucked in. Everyone gasped, and some shouted "Hey!" or made other, ruder comments of sputtering amazement.

Mugoi elongated his posture as he reached the descending portion of his arc, assumed a standing position, landed feet-first on the parallel bar—and stopped. He wobbled for a second, then stood in place, extending his arms in either direction in a victory pose.

The sudden hush below him gave way to laughs, clapping, cheers, and profanity-laden exclamations. What he had done would have been functionally impossible for a regular human. Even with augmentations like his it was an incredible feat of agility and coordination.

Nasreen's alarm faded, at least in part. Everything was mostly okay, although the stunt had still been reckless and tasteless, in her opinion.

Commotion. Her eyes moved back to floor level, where a couple of beefy men were shouldering through the crowd, one in plainclothes, the other wearing a security uniform.

"Hey!" the latter bellowed, pointing upward. "Get down from there. Those beams aren't meant for that. You could bring the whole goddamn ceiling down on us! Not to mention damage the electrical systems."

Mugoi eased himself into a sitting position and allowed his legs to hang over the edge, then dangled by his arms, finally dropping to the floor below where he squatted into the impact and sprang back up to a stand. His face was nonchalant. "Pardon me. I did not see any wiring there. I had a good look at it."

The plainclothes security guy rasped, "Cute, but if you're going to pull shit like that, you're out the door. Like yeah, haha, it was a good show, great. I don't care how famous you are. We've got a lot of people in here to keep safe."

Rumblings and murmurs of anger went around the crowd. Everyone was picking a side in any potential conflict that might break out. Nasreen glanced around at the faces and sampled the vibe according to her well-honed intuition.

She decided there was no imminent danger of a brawl or other ugliness, but things could move in that direction quickly if someone wasn't willing to deescalate. The bouncers were being more confrontational than necessary. They must have skipped training on how to resolve minor situations without threatening the sorts of people who were unlikely to back down. People like Mugoi.

She cleared her throat. "We were about to leave. We have stuff to do in the morning. Mugoi, that was impressive, but we need you to save your strength for when you really need it. Braelin, Jolo, let's go."

Mugoi's inhumanly beautiful face shifted, the faint smirk changing to slight disappointment, but he was mercifully smart enough to realize that she was correct. He didn't protest.

Braelin groaned, "Aww, damn. I forgot about that part. The whole 'having things to do tomorrow' bit, I mean. Oh, well."

Neburu kept silent but led the way toward the door. The rest followed her, ignoring the bristling security guys, while half the people in the bar waved goodbye. Nasreen waved back. It was good PR.

Outside, the lights emanating from the dome's interior surface had dimmed to a deep, soft blue as they usually did when a Station entered its night cycle. The architects of humanity's new homes had determined that people would respond better to conditions that resembled the sun's rising and setting on the mother planet.

Muttering to themselves, not bothering to converse with one another in their faint disappointment and aggravation, the quartet trudged down the street away from the club.

They got about a block away when Nasreen realized she hadn't been paying attention to everything around her. Between her career as a freelance espionage agent and investigator and the Marauder training she had received from Dante, she ought to have known better. Even the best were known to forget their second natures occasionally.

She frowned, wanting to slap herself. She was not *that* drunk. A bit tipsy but hardly reeling with intoxication. The others were the same, including Mugoi. They'd had enough perhaps to dull their senses below the threshold of peak performance, but they were still functional for the most part.

One block later, there came a moment when something invisible and unspoken passed among the four of them, like an electromagnetic signal—the mutual understanding that someone was following them. The movements of a smattering of dark figures on the other side of the street, along with other individuals in nearby alleys or parallel lanes, were converging in a fashion far too perfect to be coincidental.

Nasreen took a sharp left at the next alley. It was empty, short enough for them to clear it quickly, and a broader and better-lit street lay at the other end. There was a chance that their pursuers might cut them off if they moved fast enough, but she decided it was worth the risk.

The apprentices took the hint, falling in behind her with only a second's hesitation. They also said nothing but continued murmuring between themselves. It sounded like Braelin and Neburu were chatting about something from the club.

Beneath her dread and alertness, Nasreen had to admit she was proud of them. They had grasped that a serious situation was developing and slid into the role of dealing with it without her needing to slap them into shape or tell them to keep quiet and avoid giving themselves away.

She strode down the alleyway at increased speed, a trot verging on a jog but keeping her footfalls as silent as she could. The haze of alcohol, slight though it had been, had vanished from her mind as necessity dictated. She could only hope that it had not dampened her reflexes to any appreciable degree.

They emerged into the street beyond and saw silhouettes closing in from all sides in their peripheral vision. A rapid backward glance confirmed their pursuers from behind were advancing down the alley. They were surrounded.

Under her breath, feeling the uptick in tension between the four as they readied themselves, Nasreen muttered, "Here we go..."

CHAPTER FIVE

Dante left HQ behind about half an hour after Nasreen, Braelin, Neburu, and Mugoi had departed. He wanted a brief period of peace and quiet to recharge his brain before he set out on his second mission of what had been a long day. He didn't expect it would take too long. If he did everything right, it could be a relatively simple in-and-out procedure, one that came with certain risks attached.

Then again, *everything* had potential risks. Eleven people died in a freak shuttle crash less than a week ago. The authorities were still investigating the cause, but it seemingly had resulted from a long chain reaction of minor mistakes and mechanical failures that had finally added up to something disastrous. Shuttle travel was safe, for the most part. Safer than traveling by car back on Earth in the old days, according to the official studies published on the subject. There were no guarantees in life, except that sooner or later, it always ended.

Dante had no intention of allowing his life to end anytime soon if he could help it. He suited up as if he expected to encounter mild to moderate resistance on a stealth job. Enough stuff to give him adequate protection and a couple of possible contingency plans, but not enough to draw undesired attention to himself.

"Attention," he muttered as he checked to ensure his knife was still in its sheath. "I keep forgetting I was streaming on fifty million screens not that long ago."

It was a rhetorical comment, but Midas answered it anyway. *"True enough, sir, but consider the following. It is relatively uncommon for people to recognize you in public. Many people who notice your face vacillate about whether they should approach you or say anything. It's as though they were trying to decide if they saw Dante Shale or simply another man who is vaguely similar."*

Dante shrugged. "True." When in public, he had a way of moving and carrying himself that tended to deflect attention. Unless they were in a position to examine his face from close range, people's gazes tended to pass over him without too much extra thought. They saw only a trim, average-sized man who looked too intense to bother harassing or chatting up but otherwise unremarkable.

He did a standardized walkthrough survey of the building to ensure everything was in a proper state, then exited via the side door. He locked up behind him and armed the security systems. They could afford top-of-the-line tech in that regard.

It had been one of the few expenditures Nasreen hadn't had to talk him into. He had leapt at the opportunity. He did not hesitate or waffle when there was a firm and obvious practical reason for shelling out money.

Leaving HQ behind, he headed to the nearest shuttle bus platform. A good two dozen people had gathered there, and the next shuttle would arrive in less than three minutes. He'd timed it almost perfectly. He didn't like to rush where public transportation was concerned but wasn't fond of standing around waiting.

Once the sleek vehicle arrived on its magnetic track, gliding to a smooth stop, Dante piled into the rear car along with half of the other assembled riders. The compartment was moderately crowded. There wasn't much space, but neither were they packed shoulder-to-shoulder.

It was too crowded so far to carry on a detailed conversation with his AI. He could speak mentally, but his lips often moved as he mouthed the words. Better to be safe. He waited as the shuttle looped around his destination once, riding the bus for longer than necessary to allow the car to clear out. The herd normally thinned as the night wore on.

Half of the riders were gone when they approached the place for the second time, and Dante had an entire corner to himself. Good. He looked out the windows at the camera.

The communications relay he sought was in a small substation connected to the outside of the Atlantica Central hub. It extended from the domed hull into the gravitational field beyond like a mushroom growing from the side of a tree trunk. It was common for technical facilities to be kept separate from the main Station, but less so with *communications* facilities. Some experts felt that external comms relays like this made it easier to send and receive signals from other Stations.

There was a slight problem or two, nothing unaccustomed. Places like the substation were not typically open to the general public. It wasn't *too* suspicious for a random civilian to wander up to one with questions, complaints, or the like, but Dante would require a degree of access that exceeded mere legality.

Fortunately, he was gaining more experience with such things all the time. There was always his AI to help, now that they could talk.

"Midas, as soon as we get close enough, start scanning every-thing, and I do mean *everything*. We're probably going to need to bypass multiple layers of security. Not only the alarms and all that sort of bullshit, but also the surveillance system. Especially stuff designed to detect your network connections and AI signa-ture. Block all of it and do it as quietly as you can without making a mess. I'll be able to handle some of the more physical activities."

Which included breaking things, if need be. Or putting the guards out of commission. Simply avoiding them would be better.

Paradoxically enough, the AI's inner voice sounded subdued and enthusiastic. "Yes, sir, that will be quite the challenge, but I think I'm up to it. You've done well lately at equipping me with nearly all of the tools I will need to pull off such a vast range of responsibilities."

The word *nearly* stuck out. Dante had a dim recollection of some or another app or upgrade that Midas had requested, but he had yet to shell out the money for. The AI's hunger and greed for such extravagances were bottomless. In all fairness, he put them to good use—most of the time.

As they once again approached the stop closest to the substation, Dante dismounted and strolled toward a shadowed corner where he could disappear in one of at least three directions. Other passengers disembarked and drifted off. Once they were gone, he slipped around a corner and made his way toward the station.

Mentally, he told Midas to activate the scrambler. The AI did so without bothering him with discussion, knowing it was important for his host human not to be distracted right now.

One of the recent upgrades allowed Midas to send out a mixture of visual and radio-frequency "noise." It would confound most security cameras that looked toward Dante.

A savvy human observing the camera feeds would still notice the obscuration pattern moving from zone to zone in a purposeful way and put two and two together. Still, it was enough to trip up the majority of automated security. It would make it easier to get closer to their destination without tripping any alarms or arousing anyone's interest.

The downside was that it created a strange effect in Dante's head. He could only describe it as a grinding sound, minus the "sound" part since his ears did not perceive it. It gave him a slight headache.

Gritting his teeth and trying to ignore it, the Marauder moved closer to the station. Its main access point was a large gate in the outer shell of the main Atlantica dome. A side corridor allowed expedited access for security and maintenance personnel, VIPs, and the like. Dante took the latter route. He saw no other people nearby but still moved in hunter mode, utilizing every trick in his repertoire to make himself as inconspicuous and silent as possible.

A keycode-pad protected the door. It had an advanced scrambler, but Midas was capable of hacking through it. The AI went to work while Dante stood guard. He had a wrist-mounted tranq dart launcher concealed up his sleeve that would allow him to make short work of up to two guards nonlethally. Beyond that, things could get ugly.

As Midas worked on the door, Dante reflected on how good it felt to be back to Marauding. Violence was still a frequent part of his job but not a *necessary* one. Stealth, wits, and luck often precluded it. He was experienced enough as a fighter that he'd done well during his stint as a Reaper, but he disliked the idea of being a de facto hired killer.

The door *clicked* open after flashing a brief blue-green light to indicate that all was well. Dante slipped in and gently shut it behind him. Beyond lay a short, empty, silvery corridor.

The scrambler was still in effect since his headache had yet to go away. He heard footsteps at the juncture up ahead and hung back, waiting. When a woman in a blue uniform passed ahead of him, facing away, he brought up his hand and shot her in the left buttock with one of his two darts.

She let out a short "Uh!" and tried to turn toward him, but she was already slumping toward the floor. Her eyes went glassy as the fast-acting tranquilizer raced through her bloodstream.

Dante caught her mid-fall and dragged her deeper into the facility, depositing her unconscious body in a maintenance closet to get it out of sight.

From there, he passed into an area that was less "clean" in its structure, with protruding pipes, wires, and the like everywhere, the typical look for a part of any Station that the general public never saw. When another security patrol approached, Dante jumped, grabbed two pipes, and hoisted himself into the shadowed lattice of junk above the hallway, grunting with effort.

The guards passed beneath him. He couldn't tell if they were specifically looking for him yet. Their gait was quick and purposeful, but nothing indicated they were on high alert. At worst, they may have been investigating a minor anomaly.

Exhaling, Dante lowered himself and dropped to the floor. He'd stayed in good shape, but he wasn't as young or strong as he used to be, and he vowed to start working his arm and shoulder muscles more in the coming weeks.

Five minutes later, after sneaking through a miniature labyrinth of short hallways and narrow tunnels, he came to the room that housed the substation's main comms relay. Midas had already been working to access the code and delivered it to Dante's brain right on time.

Sending the AI a faint emotional signal of approval, Dante punched it in, ducked through the door, and entered a circular room with a columnar console at its center. There were two alcoves stuffed with random machinery off to the sides, which would make acceptable places to hide if necessary.

He approached the console and clicked on the main interface button. While waiting for it to boot up and for Midas to scan and analyze it, he took out his knife and used its blade to pry open a panel beside the screen and look at the hardware. What he saw was significant, and glancing back at the screen, the reams of information that scrolled past confirmed his suspicions.

The Station had constructed the relays to allow for easier

message-sending between one Station and another, without the usual interference that went with trying to beam things around a curved trajectory through space. Or in extreme cases, sending them around the Earth toward Stations on the planet's opposite side.

"Shit," he muttered, barely articulating the word under his softened breath. His mind ran through the mass of data, imposing order and making sense of it.

Someone had added multiple extra processing units, greatly increasing the amount of data the relay could handle and the speed at which it would manage it. Furthermore, they had installed various boosters that would increase the signal power by an enormous degree. With that much augmentation, there was no doubt the relay could send communications down to Earth's surface.

He moved on to the relay's message logs, with Midas silently grasping his purpose and unlocking the more advanced inner security measures while Dante worked at hacking through the outer ones. Together, they breached the system's defenses in minutes.

Dante stared at the screen as further reams of information popped up. Quite a bit of the relay's activity seemed innocuous or normal. Not all. Some were connected to operations still running Dirtside. Things with no official clearance numbers or other data attached to them—so-called "black site" projects, taking advantage of the lax oversight on Earth to dodge the laws back home in the Stations.

Said operations were directly connected to networks in multiple city hubs in orbit. Atlantica Central was not the only one.

Mouthing the words but speaking mostly within his mind, Dante commanded, *"Midas, start downloading all the locations and frequencies related to Earth-bound activity."*

"At once, sir." The AI got to work.

Based on experience harvesting data from similar consoles, Dante estimated that the process would take two to three minutes, depending on the strength of the relay's encryption and the amount of info for Midas to take.

About a minute and a half had passed when Dante's vision suddenly turned white, as though a flash-bang or incendiary shell had gone off in front of his face.

He staggered back two steps, breath hissing between his teeth as he sharply inhaled and put his hands to his eyes. It took him a second to realize that he could see perfectly. The white flash was within his mind, a hallucination affecting his physical perceptions without being directly related to them.

Midas had gone silent. As he tried to recover, Dante recognized the telltale signs of his AI's abrupt disablement, and his gut clenched with fear. The situation reminded him of when an EMP grenade hit him, but not as severe.

He looked around. There were no obvious signs of trouble in the external, material world. Whatever had happened was restricted to the domain of network signals and frequencies.

"Midas," he whispered. "Are you okay?" The console before him looked no different than it had a couple of minutes ago. His skin crawled. It would have been less disturbing if the screen *had* changed. At least he'd have some idea of what was going on.

Then a light flicked on in his brain. The AI came back online, reactivating the synapses to which he was connected.

The cultured, British-accented voice stated, "Terribly sorry, sir, but I had to shut down for safety reasons. I hit something along the lines of a highly sophisticated firewall that possessed a powerful counterattack. If I had remained in operation, it would have overloaded me to the point of causing intense heat generation that could have resulted in severe physiological damage to your brain."

Dante's eyes narrowed, and his jaw clenched. "I see. Thanks for that, then."

He had heard of such programs. They were rare, expensive, and massively illegal except for certain restricted uses rarely granted by any Station's government. Not only because they were typically fatal to the persons affected but also because of the danger of them being pirated and distributed to unscrupulous hackers or other miscreants.

The majority of the Stations' population had implants of one type or another. If not AI, then at least minor medical implants, security biometrics, and the like. The security program they'd triggered used a kind of encoded virus that attacked all such devices. Their abuse could, in theory, injure or kill enormous numbers of people.

Reading his thoughts, Midas explained, "Yes, it was one of those, I'm afraid. Whoever owns and operates this Station either has extremely high-level access or is most unethical but good at covering their tracks and bribing or threatening anyone who examines their activities too closely."

Dante was about to ask after more of the details since knowing about the relay's security might be nearly as useful as downloading the info on its communications with Earth. Then he heard footsteps.

Shifting instantly into combat mode, Dante sprang toward one of the alcoves. Midas highlighted a loose panel along one of the walls, which he pried free, embedding himself within a mass of wiring behind it and replacing the panel. A cooling vent within it allowed him a view of the console chamber.

A small group marched in. They stopped in unison before the glowing column. Dante had a good look at them. He did not keep his eyes on them for long, but the brief impression was enough to reveal several important yet contradictory facts.

First, there were four men. That seemed like one or two too many. All of them wore the standard Atlantica Central Utilities blue uniforms, so nothing about that was suspicious in and of itself.

However, the individuals wearing the uniforms did not seem quite right. It was difficult to put his finger on precisely what about them felt "off" to him. It was simply a hunch, a function of well-honed intuition and many years of experience recognizing problems before they developed.

Utility employees were almost always a mixed bag. If four of them were to turn up somewhere, he would have expected two or three older, grizzled persons in questionable physical condition, one green kid gawking at everything, and perhaps one other "wild card" employee.

These four were oddly homogeneous. All were between the approximate ages of twenty-seven and forty, physically fit and grim-faced, with an air of cold professionalism. They seemed less like men on a job than men on a *mission*.

They surveyed the scene before them. One out front said, "Supposed to be a dead body here. Either it's a false alarm, or someone sent a goddamn KR4 in here."

"Could be." The guy behind him sounded skeptical. "Some of the saboteurs they hire these days aren't *only* techie geeks."

The others weighed in, each offering his professional opinion on what was happening. They seemed oddly unbothered by the prospect, which must have occurred to them, that someone had broken in but was hiding in one of the alcoves.

The usage of "KR4" caught Dante's attention at once. There was an off chance it was an arcane technical term known only to those who repaired the intricate machinery that filled the bowels of the Stations and the equipment rooms of high-tech offices and facilities. He doubted it, especially given the way the man had said it. He was using it in the context of human fatality.

"KR" followed by a number was common lingo among Reapers, freelance security who worked high-risk jobs, and mercenaries. It referred to a given individual's kill ratio, with the numbers corresponding to blocs of percentages. A violence-oriented professional with a rating of four was one who regularly ended the lives of at least seventy-five percent of his opponents in armed conflicts. Dante had acquired a KR4 about six years ago and had yet to return to a KR3.

Other things told him these guys were probably not employed by the utility firm. Minor details of how they moved, their clipped and hushed manner of speaking, and the undertone in their voices as they discussed the prospect of finding a corpse instead of a living man. All suggested they were jaded when it came to death.

Plunderers, military veterans, and former law enforcement officers often spoke in such a way. The sorts of individuals most likely to fill out mercenary roles.

The first man who'd spoken, apparently the leader, remarked, "Okay, fine. We know what to do."

He and the other three produced batons that looked like the standard truncheons often used by baseline security personnel. With the flick of a button, the batons transformed themselves into something else entirely. Carbon filament blades extended from the sides of the baton's heads and the tips, forming a slight crescent shape. Each weapon became like a hand ax or short scimitar. The material in their weapons was sharp enough to cleave through bone with minimal effort and specifically intended to be lethal.

All four men piled into the alcove opposite the one Dante hid in. Their refusal to divide their force once again marked them as dangerous professionals. However, they left Dante an opening to slip behind them and out the door. Unless they had sealed the entrance using an emergency procedure, which was possible.

If that were the case, Dante would have to fight the whole quartet to get out of the room, let alone the substation. His odds were not looking the best.

Midas offered gently, "I will do what I can to increase our chances. I'm afraid the situation is grim, isn't it?"

It was unnecessary to reply in words.

Dante slid the panel aside and crawled out from amid the wires. His long experience at prowling around Dirtside enabled him to keep quiet. He was almost free when he heard the door slide open again and another group marched in. Eyes bulging, Dante pressed himself back against the wall and tried to stay out of sight.

Four more men appeared. They were dressed like generic private security contractors of middling ability. Behind them was the blue-uniformed woman whom Dante had tranquilized and stuffed in the closet. She reeled in place, conscious but disoriented and twitchy, probably due to being given a fast-acting stimulant to counteract the dart.

"Hey!" the guy out front shouted. "Since when do you assholes have clearance to be in here? Who sent you?"

Dante noted that these guys appeared to be a notch or two down the totem pole from the first group. Their weapons were largely nonlethal, intended to injure or incapacitate—tranq-spike razorfists, stun batons, and the like. Their armor was serviceable but nothing special.

One of the fake utility employees emerged from the other alcove, holding his carbon-bladed baton with casual assurance. "You don't work here. We might as well ask you the same question. We're looking for a saboteur."

"Bullshit," the leader of the other group shot back. "He's ours. Clear out of here, now."

The other three mercs emerged from the alcove and simply attacked. They lunged forward, unspeaking, aiming to kill the intruders quickly so they could return to their search. One of the goons in the second group cried in shock, and everything became a grinding, thrashing maelstrom of violence. The dazed woman in the rear flattened herself against the wall and screamed.

Dante whispered to himself, "Now." He ducked out and made for the door.

One man from each group noticed him at the same time, and

both leapt toward him, recognition flaring on their faces. Dante moved toward the guy from the second group, caught his arm holding a stun baton, and manhandled him in between himself and the killer from the first quartet.

The carbon filament blade sheared through the armored vest and sank into the man's midsection. He gasped in pain. Dante directed his arm holding the baton into the assassin's head so the force of the blow combined with the electrical shock knocked the man on his ass, disabled or possibly dying. Both collapsed together in a tangled mass of limbs as Dante sprang free, heading for the door.

Another of the men from group two noticed him and tried to break free of the brawl with group one. Dante ducked under his clumsy attack, punched him in the back of the knee, and hurled him back into the melee, so his stumbling body blocked off the rest of them for a precious second.

He reached the exit's threshold. The female guard came to her senses and clawed at his eyes. He shouldered her aside and threw her into the wall. Her forehead *clunked* against the surface, and she dropped unconscious for the second time that night.

Dante jogged down the corridor and went straight for the substation's side entrance. By this point, getting out undetected was probably impossible, but with all the commotion he might still squeeze through.

To his surprise, another blue-uniformed figure lay shuddering in a heap, with a small bloody hole in the thigh. Group two had tranq-stabbed him and left him there.

"Fuck," Dante muttered. Everything clicked together at once.

He opened the side door and emerged back into the main Atlantican structure. The door had been disabled through brute force, saving him some work. A couple of civilians had stopped to gawk. Dante ignored them, pushing one aside and ducking into a shadowy lane, then an alley.

The second group had nothing to do with the substation or its personnel. They had followed him the whole time, tracking him to the relay, only to crash into the fake security gang unexpectedly.

If someone had sent goons after him, they had probably sent a similar group elsewhere.

Dante pulled out his sphere and speed-dialed Nasreen. The signal hummed away for far too long. Nasreen always answered within a minute or less.

Ever the observant type, Midas commented, "Oh, dear. Perhaps she is in trouble, too?"

Dante's nostrils flared. "Yeah. Probably."

CHAPTER SIX

Nasreen fell into a subtle fighting stance as a tall, broad-shouldered man stepped out in front of them, assuming the role of spokesman for the group who'd surrounded the four clubbers. She angled her body toward him with her feet spread and knees slightly bent. It wasn't too obvious, but a sufficiently well-trained or experienced opponent would grasp at once that she had prepared for violence.

The tall man came partially into the light. His helmet's visor blocked full view of his face, but Nasreen realized he was a stranger. He wore the type of midrange gear favored by respectable but unextraordinary private security contractors. Of his various companions, about half had dressed similarly, and the other half in plainclothes.

Nasreen estimated their total numbers at twelve, maybe sixteen. Three or four of them to each member of her group. The ones openly in uniform were wearing razorfist gauntlets, but they hadn't deployed the knives within them. She suspected they were backup weapons of last resort. Instead, they all seemed to favor stun batons, tranquilizer prods, or simple clubs.

More disturbingly, four of them, all from among the plainclothes agents, were carrying small purse-like objects that Nasreen finally recognized. Portable nets that could deploy a snare big enough to envelop a large human and immobilize them with a mixture of disruptive sonic pulses and chloroform fumes. They were popular with professional kidnappers.

These men had not come to kill them. They probably weren't too concerned with whether or not their quarry came out of the encounter in peak health, though.

Nasreen said to the others in a low but sharp voice, "They're using nonlethal."

Mugoi snorted. "We noticed. Or at least I did."

Before Nasreen could chastise him for turning *this* situation into a competition, the tall guy out in front spoke. "There's nowhere to go, and we greatly outnumber you. You're coming with us. It's up to you if you want to do it the easy way or the hard way. You won't like the hard way. Trust me."

Braelin let out a long, resigned sort of sigh. He stretched his arms, cracked his neck, and drawled, "Well, if those are our only options, I guess we have no choice but to—"

He interrupted himself by springing forth with surprising speed and driving his elbow straight into the face of the nearest plainclothes goon. The man's nose *crunched*, spewing blood, and he fell back groaning in pain.

"Tell you all to fuck off," Braelin finished.

Then it began. All the attackers piled in at once, ready to overwhelm the four with superior numbers and equipment. Adrenaline surged, but Nasreen's heart still sank. They might be doomed, but these bastards would not take them without a fight.

Mugoi pounced almost horizontally onto the alleyway's corner, then zigzagged back, clotheslining one of the guys in uniform hard enough to crush his throat. He fell backward to the ground, flopping erratically. The cyborg was jumping over the head of another by the time anyone knew what was happening.

He caught a lamppost and vaulted toward the flank of the whole group.

Nasreen rasped, "Goddammit! We need to stay together!" She drew a set of brass knuckles, fitted them over her hand, and punched a man under the arm when he tried to club her in the head. It was enough to stun him for a second, so she caught his arm, swept his leg, and threw him to the ground.

Neburu stomped on another man's foot and pushed him aside, stepping closer to her friends.

Braelin remained in place as someone's razorfist blade shot out of its gauntlet and cut a long gash along his thigh. "Fuck!" he sputtered, hopping back on his good leg. He landed a decent punch to the perpetrator's bicep, knocking his arm back.

Mugoi had felled another of the kidnappers and somersaulted over the shoulders of another, coming back toward his trio of companions. He'd been reckless, but at least he used something resembling strategy. He was trying to weaken the enemy flank so the four of them, once regrouped, could break through that part of the formation.

Two men came after Nasreen and Neburu in a flurry of swinging batons and prods. Nasreen went low, grabbed the ankle of one, and sent him crashing into his friend while Neburu went high and swatted the other man in the temple as he lost his balance. Both collapsed against each other in a heap, blocking off the others from being able to mount an immediate attack.

Someone was coming up behind the wounded Braelin. Mugoi ran in at the last second and broke the man's wrist. Braelin swung around, grabbed him by the head, shoved it back into another lamppost, and sent the attacker reeling and fumbling into the masses of his fellows. Then Mugoi took a club to the shoulder that interrupted his momentum and left him standing awkwardly in front of a man who'd fallen into a defensive stance.

The defender, one of the guys in uniform, brought up his forearm. A gauntlet sheathed it. Nasreen realized too late to shout a warning that it had a certain accessory she recognized. Mugoi probably would not have heard of or paid attention to it since he focused more on bodily augmentations and weapons than conventional gadgetry.

Two glowing lines appeared lengthwise on the gauntlet and spread up and down, forming a holographic mirrored rectangle that reflected all light from the space in front of the goon. Enough gravitational and sonic force imbued it to have a semblance of solidity, but its chief function was illusion.

Mugoi exclaimed, "What kind of stupid trick is that? You think I don't know you're hiding right behind it?" Enraged by this insult to his intelligence, he stormed forward, intending to take the man on by brute, direct force.

Nasreen was still struggling against the plainclothes kidnapper who held her arm but cried, "Mugoi, no!"

From behind the illusory shield, another of the men in casual dress deployed his portable net around the hologram's edge. The device's tendrils shot out, using advanced smart seek technology to locate their target and its likely egress paths.

Mugoi grasped what was happening, but not quickly enough. He backpedaled, pivoted, and tried to lunge to the side, but the net had already spread beyond his field of movement. It closed around him, enfolding him like the tentacles of an octopus, and the air around him shimmered as the net activated its sonic and gaseous incapacitation capabilities.

Despite his augmentations, Mugoi was not impervious to such things. He slumped to the ground as the device tightened around him, and the smirking operative moved in to drag him out of the fight.

Then there were only three to continue it on Nasreen's side.

Braelin ground his teeth against the pain of his injured leg as he heaved the man in front of him against another of the kidnappers. Someone else ducked in and whacked his thigh with a club.

The cowboy faltered, falling to one knee as the leg spasmed

with pain. He lashed out with his fist and caught the truncheon-wielder with a glancing blow across the jaw, enough to buy himself a moment to get to his feet.

He failed. His legs collapsed under him, and two men piled atop him, kicking and beating him and tying his hands behind his back before pulling him aside.

That still left ten or more to move against Nasreen and Jolo. The two women inched closer together, their eyes wild and teeth bared, as their foes closed in from three sides.

Neburu muttered, "Ms. Joelle, I do not think we can win this one. I am willing to try if you are. Breaking free and running may be our only bet."

Nasreen could not reply before one of the abductors who overheard the comment sneered, "You're not breaking free of a goddamn thing. Why don't you make everyone's life easier and come along quietly?"

Neburu responded by lunging forward and drawing a razor-blade she kept up her sleeve. She kept it sheathed to protect herself not only from being cut by the exceedingly well-honed blade but from the nerve toxin she put along its edge.

The man who'd spoken must have expected a direct assault since he puffed himself up and leaned forward to intercept her, intending to crash against her and win the struggle through sheer strength. Neburu whirled and pranced aside at the last instant, whipping the blade's edge along his lightly protected side. The material of his vest split open and left an oozing red line where it passed.

Neburu went after the next man in line, already flicking the razor at him while the first one froze, his muscles paralyzed by the toxin, before toppling face-first to the pavement.

Nasreen blocked a couple of tentative strikes from two men moving closer to her. She noticed with rising panic that in her effort to take the fight to the enemy and pierce through their ranks, Neburu was getting too far afield.

"Pull back!" Nasreen yelled. "They're going to close in and flank you." She kicked the guy nearest to her in the groin. He was wearing a cup so it didn't do much harm. She did have a good angle to smash her hip against his midsection and throw him off-balance. A fast palm to the chin sent him toppling.

There were others. Half a dozen and more, all ready to swarm over her.

Neburu's drive forward had faltered. She cursed wildly in her native language as someone seized her arms and twisted them. The razor fell from her grasp. Another shoved a shock baton into her stomach. She foamed at the mouth from the shock, and the guy holding her jumped back spewing profanities.

Another operative deployed his net. It wrapped around the stunned woman, hiding her from sight and taking her out of the battle.

Nasreen landed a lucky kick to the face of the first man to lunge at her, cracking his helmet's visor and sending him faltering to his knees. She had a second, at most, to assess her chances before the entire remainder of the force engulfed her.

There was no way to win the fight. It was impossible for her to overcome the remaining attackers by force and turn the tide of the brawl. Her only options were to flee or to allow herself to be captured and hope for the best.

Since the apprentices were all being taken alive, there was hope to rescue them later. There was a chance that she, ideally with Dante's help, could break them out as long as she remained free. The choice was obvious.

Nasreen ducked under the nearest man's attempt to seize her in a bear hug, punching him in the hip as she slid by. It didn't do much damage, but it was enough to throw him off-balance for a second, buying her the time to sprint toward the nearest alley, ahead of the whole group.

"Hey!" one of them bellowed. "She's getting away. Fucking get her, *now!*"

Nasreen pumped her legs. Her feet slammed against the street, and she silently thanked whatever muse had inspired her good judgment in wearing regular, stylish boots rather than high heels. She was tall and athletic enough that she had a good chance of outpacing them, what with her head start, as long as...

"No!" she exclaimed, throwing up her hands.

An older woman had stepped out of a door that Nasreen had not seen until now. She was oblivious to the knock-down, drag-out street fight fifty-five yards away. The woman turned slowly toward the ruckus as Nasreen pivoted to the side, avoiding a collision but losing balance and stumbling into the nearest wall.

Behind them, heavy feet pounded as at least four or five of the kidnappers pursued her, getting closer by the second.

One of them growled, "Get out of the way!" and shoved the older lady aside.

Nasreen sprang into a run, reorienting herself barely in time as the first of the goon squad reached out toward her. His fingertips raked through her hair and brushed the back of her neck.

An awful memory sprang to mind of a night when the most horrific opponent she had ever had in a long and violent career had nearly murdered her. The current struggle was not on par with *that* in terms of sheer terror. There was only the single-minded, desperate determination to escape—for the sake of her friends more than herself.

The alley she had been aiming for was now a lost opportunity. Instead, clawing along the wall as she picked up speed again, Nasreen plunged headlong into the street as a pair of cars approached.

One honked madly and swerved to avoid her. She feinted toward the second vehicle, jumped sideways back to the curb, then sprinted straight ahead.

A split-second glance over her shoulder filled her with grim satisfaction. The ruse had done what she wanted. Assuming she meant to cross the street, one of the kidnappers had jumped in after her. The first of the two cars hadn't seen him behind Nasreen. He froze in place, screaming "No!" as the vehicle struck him head-on, shattered his legs, and caused him to crash into the windshield. He rolled aside into the street, his head crushed within its helmet.

Two of the others stopped beside his body, but that left two more. They pressed after Nasreen with heaving and grunting breaths, unrelenting.

She crossed the street ahead of another car, reaching the other side at precisely the right time for the vehicle to delay her pursuers by a second or so. By then, she was hustling toward an elevated platform where commuters could hail taxis that specialized in traversing the Station's sky lanes. Below it lay a broad freeway interchange, crisscrossed by traffic from cars, buses, trains, and everything else that rolled or hovered.

Nasreen ascended the ramp to the platform. It was a dead end from most people's perspectives. She had heard something about how such fixtures were increasingly manufactured with areas of slightly weaker gravity for safety and legal reasons following an unfortunate incident involving a repairman who'd fallen to his death.

There was only one way to be sure.

One of the guys behind her called to the other, "She's trying to get a taxi."

Nasreen reached the platform, where eight or nine people uncomfortably shuffled as she charged up. Ignoring them, she went to the rail. A few cars were descending from the air, but none was close enough to flag down yet. With a glance, she confirmed that the men chasing her had reached the ramp's base. She had perhaps five seconds at most to evade them.

A shuttle bus below was slowing down for the interchange.

Inhaling and trying to ask herself what in God's name she was thinking, Nasreen vaulted over the railing and plummeted into the empty air beyond it. The people waiting for taxis screamed, and her pursuers cursed in wrathful frustration.

Nasreen's stomach churned as she fell, but her pace slowed, and everything became blurred and slower in her visual perception. Her momentum faltered, the sense of control returned, and at last she dropped onto the roof of the lightly chugging bus with no more impact than if she'd hopped onto it from six feet above.

Since it was a moving vehicle, there was still enough inertia for her to fall over and roll. She reached out and caught one of the rungs along the top, used by service personnel, and clung to it as the vehicle passed through the interchange and picked up speed again. Her gaze darted back and spotted the two helmeted men glaring at her from the platform, dwindling as the shuttle sped away.

She waited. Wind whipped by and her insides felt like liquid, but she passed the ride safely.

Minutes later, the bus reached the next stop on its route. Before any passengers emerged, a guard or foreman stepped out and immediately looked up at her. "What are you doing up there?" he shouted, half angry and half concerned.

Nasreen crawled to her knees, jumped down, and landed on her feet, but she had to fall into another roll to avoid breaking an ankle. She came out of it standing straight, ragged and flustered but otherwise unharmed.

"Sorry," she quipped and ran off before the baffled man could question her further.

The city's bustle swallowed her as she disappeared within its chaos, melding in with a crowd and slipping away into a forgotten nook between businesses.

Her apprentices were captives. She had escaped, but it wasn't much of a victory. An awful sense of sympathy mixed with near panic threatened to overwhelm her, and she pulled out her sphere, wanting to talk to Dante as much as she ever had.

She'd missed two calls from him. As her finger hovered over the button, he called a third time. She answered it at once.

"It's Dante. Are you okay?" No bullshit pleasantries, as usual. The edge in his voice suggested he hadn't had the best evening, either.

Nasreen could only gasp, "They took them. I'm the only one who got away."

CHAPTER SEVEN

In her brief conversation with Dante after they'd both calmed down and started to figure out what the hell was going on, Nasreen said they should meet at "the usual place."

This was a code. It referred to a place they had never met before, one of the many safehouses Nasreen had set up during her tenure as a spy for hire. The unassuming, middle-class condo was deep within Neo Casablanca. It wasn't too far from Atlantica Metro but far enough to be safe.

Dante opted for a middle-of-the-road transport line, one that was largely indistinguishable from many others like it. It wasn't as conspicuous as some of the higher-end ones. At the same time, it didn't give off the same air of suspiciousness as some gutter-level ones. Those were often frequented by refugees, covert operatives, fugitive criminals, and the like, in the mistaken belief that no one would stoop so low to find them.

He blended in with the motley crowd on the shuttle bus. Midas helped, drawing his attention to anyone who looked at him too closely, too long, or seemed uncomfortable with his presence. Half of the time Dante noticed them himself. The other half he did not. It made him wonder how well he could have survived without his AI. In any case, he avoided the person in question or tried to slowly move away from them, hiding his face all the while.

The bus stopped at a platform beside a broad marble avenue lined with palm trees, fountains, and Cordovan-style arches. It would have been easily mistaken for an upscale part of town if not for the average crowd milling around.

Dante wove through the streets, which were narrower than in many cities. He slipped between buildings when he could get away with it or walked normally with other pedestrians when not.

As usual, Nasreen had selected a place that was far enough away from bus platforms and train stations to offer privacy from them but within a reasonable walking distance. Dante found the condo block about fifteen or twenty minutes after he disembarked from the shuttle.

There was a gate out front, but Nasreen had sent Midas the code. The AI relayed it while Dante punched it in, then strode beyond the retracting steel barrier into a garden-like expanse.

Nasreen's small but nicely furnished condo lay near the back of the small enclosure. No other condos were in immediate sight. He nodded with satisfaction and slipped through the front door, hoping that its unlocked state meant she was already present.

"Dante," she greeted him almost instantly. Her voice held a note of relief, even joy at seeing him. "Well, I'm glad you made it and remembered the code. I thought you might go back to headquarters."

He grunted. "I remembered. We discussed it at length. If people are following us all over Atlantica Central, it probably means they're surveilling HQ. I wasn't born yesterday."

Abruptly, her demeanor shifted. She stood beside a luxurious turquoise couch, with a potted palm swaying in the air-conditioned breeze beside her, and wrapped her lean arms around her midsection. The dress she wore, the same as last night, looked good on her, but she was bedraggled and hadn't slept. Probably wasn't in the best mood, either.

She snapped, "Goddammit. If you're so wise, shrewd, and experienced, why the hell weren't you available when we needed you? You didn't notice that people were tracking us. If by some chance you *did*, you let me and our apprentices wander off by ourselves and get surrounded. There were at least fifteen of the bastards! There's only so much we can do against that many guys."

He stared back at her, seeing the hurt on her face—physical and otherwise—the determination and desperate concern for the trio taken by their mysterious enemies. It occurred to him that it may have been a maternal thing on some level. Nasreen was a professional, but she'd come to like the three trainees more and more as time passed.

Not to mention the night's excursion was her idea. She must have felt responsible.

He frowned, feeling how his expression softened as it sometimes did when he considered her emotions and discovered that surprisingly, he could understand them.

"I'm worried about them too. Like you said, the kidnappers took them alive, right? They wouldn't have done that only to kill them later.

"Assholes in old movies might try to capture people alive so they can feed them to sharks later, but real life doesn't work that way. If professionals want someone dead, they kill them. They don't fuck around. If they kept our apprentices' heads on their shoulders, it means they're saving them for something."

Nasreen sighed, impatient. "I know that. What if they torture them? Or implant something in them that turns them against us?"

It was a real possibility. He knew he had to, but Dante didn't want to think about it too hard.

"I don't know. We'll have to rescue them before that

becomes likely. Consider this. I bumped into *two* groups of assholes. One intended to terminate me with extreme prejudice. Serious guys, high-end, nobody to fuck around with. The other group was more like the ones you described who came after you."

Nasreen shrugged. "Okay? The first group was security, then? I don't see your point."

"Fake security," he corrected her. "If both work for the same employer, their goals are incompatible. That suggests we're probably dealing with two different groups or factions."

Her face grew darker as the prospect sank in.

He continued, "Maybe not. It isn't unheard of for different departments, squads, or contractors working for the same employer to bump into one another and cut each other's throats out of interservice rivalry or sheer ignorance. What's that old saying? The right hand and the left hand don't know what the other is doing. Something like that.

"That's rare. What I saw earlier doesn't fit the profile. We're caught in a crossfire if you ask me. We have two enemies, but they don't seem to like each other much if you're looking for a silver lining or whatever."

Nasreen frowned at the floor, turning over different combinations of thoughts in her head. "Dammit. We always seem to end up in entanglements like this, don't we? I suppose it comes with the territory of success.

"Your assessment sounds about right, in all fairness. Either we've got a pair of mutually hostile groups both gunning for us, or possibly it's all directed by the same people, and their various minions dislike each other enough to come to open combat. In each case, life is complicated again."

"Yeah." Dante couldn't think of anything else to add. It was what it was.

Instead, he changed the subject. "Any updates on how heavily they're surveilling us at the other places?" It would have been asinine to assume these people *weren't* watching any of their usual haunts.

She sat on the couch with a heavy, abrupt motion. "No. My deep-cover programs report 'suspicious activity' in a generic sense, and some cameras and microphones have been covered, turned off, or disabled. That includes all the ones at headquarters and maybe a third of my safehouses. Mostly the obvious ones where we've spent a lot of time."

Dante nodded. No surprises there. Whoever was watching them was being thorough about it.

Nasreen continued. "We can safely assume that all of those places are compromised, and they may be creeping in on several others as well. This one is still safe so far. There's no guarantee they won't find it in a day, a week, or a month. We'll have to be vigilant and probably stay on the move as much as possible."

Dante suggested, "Shifts. We shouldn't be asleep at the same time. One of us should be here most of the time, if we can, to warn the other if anything looks fishy. Especially if I'm right and we have *two* hostile factions gunning for us."

A ripple of tension went visibly through Nasreen's body, and she glared at him. "Maybe it would only be *one* if you weren't pursuing your little obsession, hmm?"

He stared back at her, stony-faced. She had a point, but he wasn't about to let her browbeat him when what mattered was facing the threats before them, regardless of past mistakes.

"Maybe. It would only have delayed the inevitable. You heard the Voices. They said they'd be watching us, possibly coming for us, one day. The thing you're right about is that we need to rescue our apprentices. They deserve that much. Finding them will help us get a better grasp on what the hell is going on."

Nasreen's demeanor softened as he spoke. He hadn't raised his voice or otherwise reacted to her accusations. By being a pillar of calm strength and reassuring her that he cared about

Braelin, Jolo, and Mugoi, he had taken the wind out of her anger and brought them back to the same mode of thinking.

She sighed. "I apologize for being angry and blaming you for everything. That isn't going to help. I'm so worried about them. It was horrible watching them get beaten and captured one by one.

"We were fighting at the top of our game yet it still wasn't good enough. I probably should have thought harder about taking them into an unsecured part of the city. They learned a lot from you. That's how we lasted as long as we did."

He nodded and tried to soften his expression. He wasn't good with gratitude and tenderness, but he was gradually learning more little techniques to express it. To at least show her that he was trying.

"Well, thank you. I'm not the best with, um, social cues or, you know, human interaction in general. So I should listen to you more when you've got something you're concerned about. You see things I don't. I owe you that."

She gave him one of her gentle, subtle smiles, and it touched something deep within him to a greater extent than he would have guessed.

"Okay. I'm glad you're able to say that. You're right, though. What we need to do is focus on getting the kids back. Well, they're not kids, but you know what I mean. If you're also correct about us facing at least two enemies at once, and you probably are, we're going to need help." Her smile dimmed.

Dante pulled out a chair and sat in it backward, leaning on the backrest. "Agreed. Only if it's people we can trust. We can't have someone who's compromised or sloppy about spilling info into the bad guys' laps."

"Exactly. I can think of two who...well, they might not *seem* trustworthy, but in this particular scenario they're probably the best options we have. I'll head Dirtside to find them once we work out a timetable between us."

Dante's chuckle was short and dry. "I don't even have to ask who you mean. As for what I'll be doing..." He thought it over for a moment.

During the delay, Midas spoke aloud, his voice rising high enough that both humans could hear it.

"I'll aggregate the information that Nasreen gathered from her fight with those people. She sent it to me earlier, Dante, in case I didn't mention it before. I will also scan news reports, particularly those dealing with the communications relay we visited. I ought to be able to piece something together. Is that acceptable?"

Nasreen nodded. "Sounds good to me. Dante?"

"Yeah, sure. Now that I've had a sec to think, I'll reach out to a few arms dealers and the like. The guys who came to the relay to kill me had batons that deployed lethal carbon blades. Those aren't very common. They're expensive and require skill to make good ones. Anyone who sells the damn things might know something useful."

Nasreen stood. "Okay. We have our missions. Now we'll stagger our leaving times so it's harder for anyone to follow us. We may have to leave this condo unattended, but I can beef up the security enough to let us know if it's compromised. Anything else?"

Dante considered. "A cup of coffee, please, and thanks."

She nodded and strode off to the kitchenette. "Honestly," she called over her shoulder. "I'm glad you're asking me to make it. You're the better cook, but you always make the coffee so strong that it's borderline undrinkable."

"It isn't supposed to be enjoyable," he pointed out. "It's supposed to have an *effect*." He stood and pushed the chair back in. "You know, alertness."

From beside the pot, she snapped, "Hard to be alert when you've died of a heart attack, Dante. I'll make it strong by my standards, which ought to be moderate by yours. Good enough?"

He exhaled slowly. "I suppose."

CHAPTER EIGHT

Dante stepped off the shuttle and into the familiar streets of Londonburg. He hadn't been here in a few months. It was a nice enough town, no worse than any other. He still associated it with the rigors, betrayals, drama, and difficulties of his months-long enmity with Slaine Solar Solutions.

That company no longer existed. Cormac Slaine was dead, and the firm dissolved—its assets and responsibilities bought up by its competitors with whom Dante and Nasreen were involved. Still, SSS' malignant influence had yet to completely lift from Dante's mind.

For the time being, he had other concerns specific to this town and his task for the day.

Marcus Singh was an arms dealer of some repute, at least in certain disreputable circles. Officially, nothing he produced or sold was illegal, but his clientele were mostly Plunderers, and almost everything Plunderers did fell into the Stations' legal gray area. It made him a cautious man as well as an ambitious one.

He wasn't Dante's usual source for weapons or gear. Dante preferred to use budget-but-quality equipment for temporary gigs. Otherwise, he bought wholesale parts from weapons manufacturers and assembled them himself, attuning them to his exacting standards. That was the best way to acquire the best possible weaponry. Guns he wanted to keep by his side for a long time.

Paradoxically, Singh was a frequent customer of *his*. He sometimes acted as a fence or middleman for rare or custom tech, not least stuff taken from Dirtside that might allow for modifications impossible to find elsewhere. He always had his ear to the ground for sources of such things.

If someone had recently been looking for carbon filament blade batons, Singh might well have heard about it.

Dante advanced from one of Londonburg's many bus stations with the tube that led to others far behind him and the city's great dome above and ahead. He walked across a couple of busy streets when permitted, shuffled along, and cut through alleys when he thought he could get away with it. He was no more conspicuous than any of the town's millions of passengers and pedestrians.

Someone else trudging past cast him a second glance, squinty and curious. Dante kept walking and the man vanished into the crowd streaming in the opposite direction. Probably a regular civilian who might have recognized a celebrity but couldn't be sure. Professional trackers usually weren't so obvious when they sighted who they were looking for.

Still, at no point could Dante completely relax. Not with both hostile factions still out there.

Dante's guts curdled with tension as he approached the discreet little cluster of buildings set back from a side road where Singh conducted his business. Things had gone poorly the last time he spoke to the arms dealer.

That had been right before Dante and Nasreen had taken on their three apprentices. Singh had desperately wanted them to take on a particular job that would lead to a massive haul of electronics, enough for him to make a significant surplus over his usual profit margins.

It would have involved "borrowing" a few things from a facility back on Earth that a couple of tribes of Dirtwalkers, cooperating for the first time in a generation, were using as a rudimentary water treatment plant. The tech Dante would have had to take into the place could have disrupted the facility's equipment. There was also a serious risk of provoking an ugly and unnecessary confrontation with the Dirtwalkers.

Despite the money involved, Dante had answered firmly in the negative.

Singh hadn't taken it well. He flew into a rage, spouted off unflattering and uncharitable things about Dirtwalkers, insulted Dante's character, and threatened to spread nasty rumors about him.

Admittedly, Dante could have handled it better too, given what he'd said *after* all that.

He drew a deep breath and approached the shop.

The nice thing about being famous, Dante decided, was that people already knew a thing or two about his personality. Therefore they were less likely to be shocked than they had been back when he was a nobody. True, people didn't talk about him as much as they had a year ago, but his name was still one that many people recognized. Those who had cause to discuss his existence, not to mention reason to interact with him, universally acknowledged a simple truth.

Dante Shale was blunt and straightforward to the point of unintentional rudeness, if not a social disability. A handful of psychologists had speculated about what disorders he may or may not have. He didn't *intend* to be rude. Generally, he didn't understand or have much patience for intricate niceties and decorum.

He opened the door, stepped in, and immediately stated,

"Singh. I'm *not* here to shove my fist down your throat. Okay? I promise."

The man at the desk within the office stared at him dumbly. Then a sardonic twist appeared at the corner of his mouth. "Well, well. That is encouraging, then. Who *are* you? Is there a reason I should know why you would have said that to Mr. Singh?"

Dante closed the door behind him and sighed. Usually, Singh was the only person present. Perhaps he had moved up enough in the world to afford a full-time assistant. Dante's demeanor was about halfway between casual and guarded as he approached the stranger, who remained seated.

"I'm a past customer of his. We had an argument, but I'm, uh, willing to forget about it and talk business if he is too."

The man was nondescript, about ten years younger than Singh but of similar ethnic background, and wore thick glasses. "I see. Well, you seem to be acting under the assumption that I work for him. He does not use this property anymore because he sold it to me. I still have some of his contact information, so if he is the person you are looking for, perhaps I can point you in the correct direction?"

"Sure." Dante had a faint sinking sensation in his gut. Singh did not make it easy for people to get hold of him directly. Any information the younger man might have was likely to be a front or an intermediary, making it easier for Singh to obstruct him if he didn't feel like talking. It was worth a try.

The man gave him a phone number supposedly for Marcus' new business. Dante pulled out his sphere and made the call while still in the office. He didn't want the man to be out of sight until he had a better idea of what was going on.

A woman spoke on the other end of the line. "Hello, this is Mr. Singh's office. May I help you?"

Dante cleared his throat and spoke in a slightly higher, smoother register than his usual voice. "Yes, hello, I was referred to Mr. Singh by an individual named Theo McCormack. I am interested in reviewing his most recent wares and making a purchase if he has what I am looking for."

McCormack was another mutual contact. Dante didn't know if Singh was still working with him, but name-dropping the Irishman at least meant that Singh's receptionist or assistant would grasp that she was speaking to someone who knew a thing or two about the industry and had made enough connections to get started.

"Oh, I see." The woman paused. "One moment, please. Remain on the line, if you would."

Dante bared his teeth. "Certainly." He hung up and blocked the number. Asking him to remain on the line was asking to get tracked, geolocated, and possibly hacked.

Sighing again, he muttered to the bewildered-looking guy at the desk, "Thanks but it sounds like I'll have to find him myself. Don't worry. I'm not looking to harm him or anything. Like I said, we had an argument. I need to talk to him. Do me a favor and don't warn him, or he might flee to some godforsaken place where he'd miss out on a really good business deal."

The man at the desk blinked behind his spectacles. "I believe I understand, yes. Your affairs with him are not my affairs. Good luck?"

Nodding, Dante left. Once out on the street, he looked up at the dome and reviewed his store of knowledge.

He had only the vaguest idea of where Singh's new headquarters might be. The man frequented a couple of haunts—a spa a third of the way across the city, for starters. Dante had met him there before about two years ago. If he wasn't at his new office, there was a reasonably good chance he was there.

Midas was listening in on his thoughts. *"Traffic is not suffering any major obstructions, sir, if you would like to take public transportation to the appropriate neighborhood. Walking would almost certainly be slower."*

"Thanks." He headed for the nearest shuttle platform.

The ride was uneventful and didn't suffer from holdups, but Dante clenched his hands into fists and squirmed with restless discomfort. The false start at the shop wasn't *that* big a setback, but it made him want to kick a hole through a wall. Probably because he had wanted to get this over with as quickly as possible, and now it would take longer.

The shuttle slowed down smoothly and came to a perfect stop on the tracks before a platform perhaps two blocks from the spa. At least it wouldn't be a long walk. Dante milled out with a third of the other passengers and slipped unnoticed into the throngs and streetways, moving fast and taking the most direct route. He didn't feel like zigging and zagging all over the neighborhood right now.

The spa was located behind a low wall and surrounded on three sides by the backs of buildings with few windows. Trees strategically blocked most of those. It was a moderately high-end place, so people expected privacy. The building was nice enough but unremarkable from the outside. The inside was quite a bit more luxuriant.

Dante only hoped there hadn't been a change in management or major staff turnover in the substantial time since he'd last been there. If Singh wasn't present, new employees and administrators would be less useful in tracking him down or leaving a message.

He passed through the gates after being health-scanned, an annoyance common with such places, and approached the building's front doors. They welcomed walk-ins but were known to give second-class service to unknowns or undesirables, the better to keep their client base a bit more on the posh side.

In the front lobby, which was full of plants, statues, and fountains displaying the vaguely Ancient Greek aesthetic of the place, Dante recognized the guy behind the counter. He didn't *know* him, but he looked familiar due to having been there at least once or twice before when Dante had visited.

He approached. "Hi. I've been here before. I'm looking to

spend some time in the lounge, maybe get, um, a facial. Or some sauna time. Let's go with that."

The young man blinked. "All right, sir. What's your name and information?" He didn't recognize Dante. When he took down the name his eyes widened. Like most people in general, he knew who the Hellcat was.

Dante added, "Please don't announce that I'm here. I'd like to relax rather than have people swarming all over me. There are reasons I don't stream anymore, you know?"

"Of course." The young man processed his information, then handed him a light bathrobe. "Please undress in the locker room ahead and to your left. Then you can proceed to the lounge. The sauna is adjacent."

Accepting the robe, Dante frowned. He'd forgotten that the place had a "dress code" to access certain areas. He also considered asking if Marcus Singh was present but decided against it. There was a chance that Singh would have a standing order with the staff to inform him in advance if anyone was looking for him.

Dante found the locker room, stripped, bundled up his clothes, and put on the bathrobe. He felt ridiculous in it, but at least he would look no *more* ridiculous than anyone else. Then he exited and headed down the hall, pushing through the doors into the lounge.

The place was about as he'd remembered it. A surprisingly large area, L-shaped since it wrapped around one entire corner of the building's interior, with fluted columns, ivy, fountains, and broad couches. The temperature was warm, the air humid with residual steam from the sauna. Pots of tea with cups sat on tables, and there was a selection of old-fashioned books to read under transparent polymer covers to protect them from moisture.

Dante looked around and saw no one of interest. He went to the nearest table and set down his bundled clothes—he had weapons and the like within them that he'd prefer to have close to hand if necessary rather than trust their safety to the locker room. He adjusted the hem of his bathrobe and looked up.

Twenty feet away stood Marcus Singh, similarly clad only in a bathrobe, unmoving and staring bug-eyed at Dante. He was a middle-aged man of average height and trim build, with a black beard shot through with gray streaks. His mouth had fallen halfway open.

Realizing that Dante was looking back at him and remembering his threat, Singh snapped his mouth shut. Then he spun and ran.

"Hey!" Dante shouted, starting after him. "Wait. I'm not gonna do anything, Singh. Hold the fuck on!"

Other confused and irritated patrons looked up from their tea, reading, or conversations as the two men shot past. Tables rattled with the heavy pounding of their footfalls.

As they rounded the corner, a pair of large men with shaven heads and wearing dark glasses with the obligatory robes emerged as if from nowhere. One was light-skinned, and the other was dark-skinned. Both bristled with tension and rage. Singh's bodyguards. Dante had seen the darker one hanging around the shop.

The lighter one barked, "Hey! Stop right there, pal, or *we'll* stop you."

Singh slipped between the two but nearly crashed into a couch and table where an old couple was trying to relax and had frozen at the sudden noise and commotion. Dante might still be able to catch him as long as no one delayed him.

Which meant dealing with the goons.

The darker of the two had moved in on Dante's flank while the other handled threat delivery. Dante saw what he was doing, stepped closer to the base of a nearby decorative column, and feinted to the side of it as the man moved in. The goon was overconfident in his speed and the length of his arms. He tried to reach around the column to grab Dante and throw him into the wall.

Dante moved *inside* the man's grasp, seized his wrist, and pulled his arm painfully around the column. His free hand struck at the guard's eyes at the same time. When the man reflexively tried to cover them, Dante kicked him hard in the groin and pulled his torso into the column.

Then he bolted after Singh again. The arms dealer had got clear of the couch with the old couple and was scrambling toward the rear hallway.

Dante gained on him, but the lighter bodyguard was faster than he was. One of his big hands closed around the hem of Dante's robe and ripped it free. Rather than try to retain it, Dante seized the end and leapt to the side, wrapping it around the bigger man's face and neck. Then he pounced on him, ignoring the gasps of horror from spectators at his sudden nudity.

The guard elbowed Dante in the stomach hard enough to stun him for a split second but not enough to ruin his attack. Dante jabbed him in the kidneys and backs of his knees, dropping him into a kneeling position, then picked up a teapot from a nearby table and smashed it into the man's head. The pot dented around his thick skull and sloshed its contents everywhere as the man fell over sideways, unconscious.

Singh had paused, watching the brief struggle with desperate intensity. He spun and bolted again. Dante sprang after him.

"Goddammit, Singh! I need information, that's all. Stop running away!" His adrenaline was pumping, and he was faster than Singh was.

Someone stood from a couch near the back exit to the hall and shouted, "Stop this at once! You have no right to—"

Singh shoved him aside but doing so slowed him down. Dante bowled into him from behind, and both sprawled forward, landing on the floor at the hall's threshold. Dante was in better physical condition. He bounded to his feet and stood straddling the other man, glaring down at him.

"That's it. I got your ass now. Christ, I only want you to answer a couple of questions. No, I'm not going to punch you in the mouth, okay?"

Everything had gone silent as the arms dealer looked up at him.

Then the blank, silent stare cracked apart. Singh burst out laughing, the deep, raucous tone of it jarring everyone around him out of their frozen tenseness.

"Ha, ha! Oh, this is ridiculous. Ha, ha, ha... Look at this. Look at *us!* We both might have had a better day if we had met over tea like businessmen. Let me up, please, and we shall try to make amends, yes? Allow me to check on my men. Oh, and please put something on." He gestured vaguely at Dante's lower midsection, thighs, and so forth.

Dante glanced down at himself. In all the commotion, he had barely noticed what had happened. He cleared his throat and glanced around. A man who'd been reclining on a couch nearby, watching the bizarre spectacle with a slack-jawed expression of shock, climbed to his feet and pulled a spare robe off a hanger. He handed it to Dante without getting any closer than he needed to.

"Thanks." The Marauder snatched it and shoved his arms through the sleeves before closing the robe over his front and belting it tightly.

Meanwhile, Singh had risen and gone to check on his fallen bodyguards. "Ah, good. They are still breathing, and will probably not require hospitalization, although I'm afraid I will need to give them the weekend off."

Dante ran a hand through his hair, which had become badly disheveled during the pursuit. "Yeah. Sorry about that."

Singh shrugged. "It is part of their job description. They knew the risks. Now, let us apologize to the staff for this unfortunate ruckus and attempt to enjoy ourselves and discuss business like civilized men. As I suppose we ought to have done from the beginning."

That had been Dante's intention. He didn't much feel like lounging around. Still, it was amazing that Singh had slid so readily back into his old, smooth, professional persona. Dante figured he might as well make the best of a good opportunity.

After helping the bodyguards onto a couch so they could recover, the pair walked to the edge of the chamber and met with a horrified-looking attendant.

Singh bowed his head to the woman. "I am terribly sorry. There was a misunderstanding, but we have cleared it up between us. There will be no further trouble. We will help clean up the disarray, yes?"

Grumbling to herself, the woman set out to do that, with Dante and Marcus trailing behind her and looking for things they needed to set in order. With all three working, it only took about five minutes to get the place looking mostly functional again.

As the attendant trundled off and the other patrons tried to pretend nothing had happened, Dante and Singh settled in at one of the tables, where a steaming pot of tea was still waiting.

Dante spoke first. "I don't have all day to talk, but we can spend a little time relaxing, I guess. Tea does sound kind of good." He pushed a cup toward the kettle.

"Of course it does." Singh poured him a cup, then repeated the process for himself. "Now, what was it you wanted from me again? To ask for information, I believe?"

Dante sipped. It was getting dangerously close to lukewarm but otherwise good, and it slaked the thirst he'd worked up during his exertions. "Yes. I, ah, I'm looking for someone who might be interested in a particular product that you may have handled or heard about. Don't worry. *You're* not in any trouble.

I'm looking for someone else I encountered using those same products."

The other man was intelligent and savvy enough to read between the lines. He grasped the basic implications at once.

"Ah, yes, of course. You will have to be more specific. There are no bugs or microphones in this place. The staff guarantees it, and I have it scanned from time to time to make sure.

"These other good people have no interest in our affairs, I can assure you. Simply speak in a low voice. Oh, but first, how have you been? I don't hear as much about you these days, now that you are no longer chasing the life of a *celebrity* Plunderer and have relegated yourself to merely being a *famous* one." He chortled.

Dante drew a slow, deep breath. He wanted to get straight to business. Singh was trying to bury the hatchet and create an air of normalcy—to throw off suspicion from the other people lounging around the spa and repair their business relationship. Spending a little pleasant quality time together was an investment in their mutual future.

"I'm fine."

CHAPTER NINE

Nasreen powered up the shuttle and went through the standard procedure of checking all her displays, looking for any warning lights, and making sure everything was where it was supposed to be. She paid attention to feedback from the dock facility and double-checked her route down to the Earth's surface.

Something in her stomach fluttered, and her hands seemed too sweaty. There was no point in denying it. She was nervous.

It wasn't the fact of flying a shuttle by herself that bothered her. A copilot or dedicated comms person was preferable, but managing the craft alone was not that demanding. She had done it many times in the past with this and other ships.

Nor was it the mere act of going Dirtside. That was almost always dangerous, yet the area she was heading to was among the safest places on the ravaged and desolate planet.

No. It was the prospect of *who* she was going to see—one man in particular. There were others involved as well. Her first meeting with him, seemingly long ago now, had been unpleasant. It had colored her every interaction with him since—even ones where absolutely nothing was nominally wrong and nothing bad had happened.

She would always think of him as *that* person, the one who had scared her to the point of developing clinical post-traumatic stress symptoms—and it had happened *after* she was already a hardened spy who had been in multiple life-or-death situations.

To take her mind off that, she reflected on the other individuals who awaited her. Most of them were more affable, or at least tolerable. She was legitimately curious how everyone was doing, even if her time was too limited for much in the way of conversation.

"It will be nice to see them again," she told herself, exhaling slowly. "All of them."

She glanced backward to ensure she had loaded the ship with all the proper hardware. She had. She hadn't forgotten anything.

Once the shuttle was powered up and in proper condition to fly, she gave the signal to open the bay doors and launched into space. The black void spread before her, with Earth looming ahead and the network of the various Stations spreading out irregularly to either side, looping around the planet like the enfolding branches of a great tree.

She easily piloted through the Station's artificial gravity and the brief neutral zone of open space before hitting the outer reaches of Earth's atmosphere. There was the usual tense and difficult period as friction flames engulfed the craft's nose and windshield. It was built to withstand the heat, and she had done it many times before, but something about it would always be unnerving on a deep level.

Then the roar of fire and wind subsided as the shuttle drifted into the lower reaches of the planet's air, a little above the tops of the roiling orangish-brown clouds. Nasreen descended until she was under them, preferring to navigate while closer to the ground and able to get better visual confirmation of her location.

She had gone straight down from Casablanca. Like most Stations, it was located directly above its original location Dirtside. Thus, she continued north and west from the northwest coast of Africa, seeking the island of Atlantica. When she found it, she made for the bleak and rocky shoreline where the local Dirtwalkers' commune inhabited a cluster of battered old ruins.

Adjacent to the ruins was a much newer facility operated by the Terra Restoration Group. As Nasreen got closer, someone pinged her with a message.

A voice, certainly that of a Station-born employee of the TRG, greeted her in the usual fashion. "Hello. Please identify yourself. This airspace is claimed by TRG Project 29. No Plunderer activity allowed. Again, please identify yourself. Over."

As far as Nasreen knew, it was rare for Plunderers to be brazen enough to attack the group's operations. They were large, well-connected, and well-respected in the Stations, not to mention the new laws passed within the previous year to protect the Dirtwalker population had applied to them by extension.

Nasreen gave her shuttle info, institutional credentials, and finally her name. "I'm here to speak to Raphorien and Urshielle if they're available. Not here on any sort of Marauder activity. Over."

The man spent a moment processing her information and perhaps conferring with a superior. "Okay, you're clear to land in the designated area, south of the treatment plant. Someone will be out to speak to you shortly. Out."

"Thank you, sir. Out." She ended the call and fixed on the landing field in question. It was new enough to be well-marked and perfectly visible even through the hazy mixture of dust and fog that sometimes obscured vision in this part of the world.

Nasreen descended and hovered briefly to check her safety readouts, then landed. She switched off the controls, readied herself, and stepped out the side door. She had programmed it to close behind her and reopen with a password. She'd also left the shuttle in quick start mode in case she needed to leave in a hurry. That mode would allow her to bypass some of the usual safety routines and get into the sky as fast as possible.

A figure emerged from the nearest structure. The older outbuilding was part of the hospital, which was the core of the settlement. It was a tall but bent man. He was somewhat overweight with soft features and a crown of crescent tattoos around his bald head.

Nasreen smiled as he approached. "Raphorien. Good to see you again."

He waved. "Hello Nasreen Joelle, and welcome back. I do hope you are well. If you have any ailments, I can see you directly since everyone has been healthier of late. The Terra people help us with medical concerns. Although my pride as a healer was perhaps at stake, their aid has been a blessing."

She shook her head. "No, I'm fine, but thank you. I'm mainly here to see Ambrose." She exhaled. "And Hyde."

"Ah, I understand. I suppose it deals with some affair of the Moonfolk, something beyond our knowledge or concerns. Come, let me show you the improvements we have made lately. You can see most of them on your way to the residential quarters."

Nasreen hoped it wouldn't take too long. If Raphorien meant to point things out as they walked, she would not be so rude as to complain. It *was* nice to see him again and to know that the Crescent-Marked were flourishing with TRG's assistance.

They strolled at a considerably slower pace than Nasreen would have preferred. The healer pointed out the extra medical facilities they had installed, the water treatment plant, and the greenhouse for growing crops and medicinal plants.

Other new installations included some barriers and guard towers that the Crescent-Kissed warriors used to keep an eye out for anyone who might approach with hostile intent. Their commune was not considered part of any tribe but was largely respected by all for their role as intermediaries. Any danger these days was more likely to come from Plunderers or the like.

Her mind wandered briefly. According to Dante, this man had

been responsible for caring for him and possibly saving his life after his battle with a belligerent group of Dirtwalkers in the ruins of Old Atlantica Metro on the day SSS betrayed him. Nasreen had no such personal connection to Raphorien, but she still liked him based on what she knew of him.

That was why she cringed at what she had to do. It was a good thing that negotiation and diplomacy were part of her spy portfolio.

"Raphorien," she piped up, interrupting him as he rambled on while moving at a slow and shuffling pace. "I'm sorry, but I don't have much time. I would love to stay for a social visit on another occasion, but today is not that day. I must find Ambrose and Hyde and request their help. It's a matter of some urgency. We have serious problems up in the Stations right now."

Raphorien paused and blinked. "Oh, I am sorry. I did not know. I thought you meant to stay for a while and speak to them when you could. I can tell you mean it, and I am sure your need is great. I would have told you sooner if I had understood your haste."

She tensed within at the last thing he'd said. Whatever he meant by that, it couldn't be good. "Told me what?"

"Neither of them is here at the moment. Ambrose is very skilled at controlling your sky-ships, so he took one such vessel full of needed supplies to a distant outpost of our order, on the other side of the island."

Nasreen grimaced. Flying from one end of Atlantica to the other would not take *that* long, but if Ambrose had to help unload the shuttle, it would be considerably more time-consuming. "I see. What about Mr. Hyde?"

Raphorien resumed walking toward the compound's residential part. "He is a warrior by nature. He has accompanied Urshielle on a hunt. They are tracking a band of raiders from a tribe little known to us who came to steal. They discovered how much valuable material we had here from the Terra people, so they raided a few outlying camps, then stole supplies from our main facility."

Nasreen shook her head in anger. "Those fools. I thought most people who live here understood you do work that benefits all Dirtwalkers on Atlantica and you were off-limits."

The healer sighed. "That is how it *should* be, and many of the tribes do respect us and spare us their raids. Some either live in ignorance or feel they should be able to take anything they wish unless someone stops them.

"Of late, there have been more and more such raids against us. Urshielle and her sisterhood of warriors are brave and skillful, but there are not enough of them to track down all the many people who have attacked or stolen from us. They are fighting a losing battle."

Nasreen stopped. Once Raphorien realized she was no longer following him, he also halted and looked at her with raised eyebrows.

She cleared her throat. "It makes sense to focus on the problem closest to hand. I need to speak to both Ambrose and Hyde, and if that means I have to help them, so be it. What frequency is Ambrose on? I believe Dante mentioned you have some understanding of radio..."

She wasn't too sure about that part. At times, the Dirtwalkers were more sophisticated than Station folk gave them credit for. The people of the Crescent had a crude but functional observatory even before TRG. Since the group's arrival, she imagined that Raphorien and his ilk were learning more useful things every day.

The healer said, "Ambrose wrote that information down, and I can show it to you. Follow me."

"Good." She sighed with relief. "Also, where is Urshielle's war band right now?" She refrained from explaining why she asked.

As Raphorien led them into the building and toward his office, he elaborated, "I am afraid I do not know their exact location. Only that they are somewhere in the western foothills at the edge of the great broken city.

"It is not the full war band—only Urshielle and your friend Hyde. They are hunting without support because the rest of the war band is spread thin across our various outposts and camps. There are many people to keep safe, and only so many warriors to do it."

Nasreen was impressed and concerned, and the mingling of the two emotions befuddled her. She rubbed her eyes. Although fearsome, Urshielle was only one person. Hyde had *been* fearsome, but last she had seen him, he was little more than a head and torso making do with a bargain-bin robotic skeletal frame that allowed him to totter around with only a small fraction of his former power.

Yet the two intended to take on a whole band of raiders. Nasreen wasn't sure whether to lean toward praising their bravery or chastising their stupidity.

"How good would you say their chances are, Raphorien?"

The man hummed low in his throat. "I do not know, for such things are not my specialty. Urshielle and Hyde have become close, more than you might think. When working and fighting together, they are a force that is greater than on their own. I have faith in them."

"Okay," Nasreen muttered. "You would know better than I would. That makes me feel a little better, I guess."

They passed other healers who eyed Nasreen with benign interest and pushed into Raphorien's office. He found a scrap of paper with Ambrose's handwriting scrawled all over it and handed it to the spy.

"Thank you." She looked around. "Radio?"

Raphorien waved her toward a room at the other end of the hall. "I should check on a patient, but I will be nearby if you need further aid. I wish you luck."

She nodded and let him go, heading toward the comms room.

Within was a radio setup that was on the primitive side but perfectly functional. It was probably an older model from the TRG. Too new to have come with the old hospital, but over a decade out of date by Station standards.

Nasreen mumbled, "Okay. Ambrose first, then after I find him, we'll worry about Hyde and Urshielle. He can help me locate them." Tracking down a pair on foot with a shuttle would be easier than the reverse.

She dialed in the frequency and spent about two minutes pinging and messaging the pilot, waiting for a response. At last, Ambrose's familiar, slightly morose voice came through.

"Greetings, this is Igento. Who is calling and what do you want? Over."

The sound of his voice raised mixed emotions. Nasreen had never particularly *liked* the man—particularly since he'd betrayed Dante *twice*—but he wasn't too offensive in person most of the time, and she had some decent memories associated with him.

"Hi, Ambrose, it's Nasreen Joelle. I'll assume you remember me. I need your help with something, and yes, it's pretty serious and urgent. Where are you? Over."

"Ah, I am at Sunrise Camp, as they call it. You can guess in which direction that is. I am doing a supply drop. What is the matter? Also, um, I hope you are well. Over."

She noted the faint tremor in his voice. Part of him may have been happy to hear her, but he correctly assumed she wanted him to do something difficult and unpleasant. He was unlikely to look forward to it. Then again, their connection was a bit patchy so she might be reading too much into it based on the wavering sound quality.

"I would rather tell you in person. Any chance you can come back to the Restoration Group's compound ASAP? It would be better not to wait long. Over."

He grumbled wordlessly, then spoke up. "There are things I

must finish or people will be at risk. Yes, I will hurry back as soon as I finish. Out."

He ended the call, putting a preemptive stop to any effort she might make to extend the conversation. Her gut clenched in mild annoyance. She supposed he had told the truth about needing to finish what he was doing before he could be bothered with her.

The only thing to do was wait.

Hours passed. Nasreen met with Raphorien again and allowed him to show her the rest of the compound, completing his tour of the new improvements. Her mind wandered, wondering if she should fire up her shuttle and try looking for Hyde by herself, simply flying around the western hills until she spotted something. That would take a lot of fuel for a task with only a slight chance of success.

As night gathered on the horizon, no shuttle came forward to request a landing. Instead, a woman in one of the guard towers—one of only a handful who had remained behind to guard the base—shouted a warning that someone was approaching on foot.

Nasreen had been lounging around in the hall near the front entrance when she heard the cry. "What the hell?" She gasped. She checked to ensure that she still had a pulsecore pistol under her jacket, then headed out the doors to observe the newcomers and assist if need be.

The woman in the tower turned a big, old-fashioned spotlight to illuminate the approaching pair. At first, it looked like one person, but it was two. The second hung draped over the back and shoulder of the first.

Nasreen marveled at the bizarre sight, nothing like what she might have expected. At least it wasn't anyone from the raider tribes.

Urshielle trudged forth, her powerfully built body showing obvious signs of fatigue. She stumbled along with barely enough strength to make it home.

On her back was Hyde. The once huge man, still reduced to a

shell of his former self, had lost an arm. Again. The one that remained dangled over Urshielle's shoulder and clutched a short-barreled rifle with a confidence that suggested he wasn't *too* badly wounded. His bestial face twisted with subdued pleasure, and his wild reddish hair swayed in the growing night breeze.

It was plain as day that the two had been in battle. They gave off an intangible vibe that announced it easily to anyone familiar with violence. Their weapons looked well-used, and bloodstains spattered them. A sense of relief emanated from them as they crossed the threshold into the compound.

Nasreen noticed that Urshielle was dragging something behind her—a small gravity sled, loaded with what must have been the last of the stolen supplies, re-scavenged from the bandit tribespeople she and Hyde had undoubtedly killed or driven off.

A Crescent-Crowned healer whose name Nasreen didn't know emerged from somewhere behind and came up by her side. "Ah," he mused, watching the pair approach. "They recovered some of it. Not much. That is only a small fraction of what the raiders took. It is better than nothing."

"Yes, I suppose so." Nasreen drew a deep breath. The pair were such a grim sight that she felt nearly guilty about the prospect of begging them for help.

Nonetheless, she strode forward to meet them.

Urshielle spotted her immediately, and Hyde a half moment later. Their eyes brightened with recognition and Nasreen waved at them.

"Hello there. I'm glad to see you made it back. May I help you?"

Urshielle huffed, "Good day, Nasreen Joelle. I am happy to see you, but I am tired. I do not need help. Hyde will be off my shoulders very soon, no matter what you do. Thank you, the offer is kind. Take this back to the hospital instead."

She pulled the sled forward, and Nasreen took hold of its handle, bringing it back toward the building. Halfway there, a healer and a TRG worker appeared, nodded their thanks, and assumed charge of it. They poked through the supplies as they moved.

Then another of the healers brought out an old wheelchair from within the main hospital building. With some help and easing from Nasreen, Urshielle lowered Hyde into it. He sat there glum-faced, tired, and oddly pitiful.

Urshielle said, "I will leave the two of you to talk alone. There are things I must see to. Hyde must be treated soon for his new injuries. Then we shall all be busy. Things are dire for us now."

She strode off with a curt nod. A new desperate vitality animated her lean-muscled frame. She had been fighting and running all day, yet there was still too much work to flag in her commitment before she retired for the night.

Nasreen looked down at Hyde. "Hyde, Dante and I need your help."

He grumbled, "You can see me. You see the shape I'm in. I wouldn't be much use to you without Urshielle to tote me around like a goddamn sick child. You heard what she said, too. She doesn't have time to leave her duties down here, and I don't think she would abandon her people even if she *did* have time. That's how she is. So unless you've got some sort of miracle lined up, well, don't get your hopes up, *chica*."

She delayed before responding, considering his words and giving him a moment to simmer down. Then she allowed a slow smile to spread. "I *do* have a miracle lined up. You ought to have a look."

He glowered at her as though not comprehending her words at first. The exertions of what must have been a long day weighed on his mind. Then his eyebrows rose. "Yeah? What?"

Nasreen took the handles of the wheelchair and pushed Hyde back to the shuttle, thankful for the built-in ramp that deployed along with the door. As they reached the threshold, Hyde suddenly stuck out his good arm and caught the edge, stopping them dead.

"Hold it," he snapped. "What's in here? I didn't agree to *go* anywhere so don't think you can kidnap me and take me off-world."

Nasreen's patience was waning, but the man had a point. "I'm not taking you anywhere, Hyde. It's easier to bring you in than to bring *it* out."

It occurred to her out of nowhere that she had almost no fear of him left. *He* was the one who had terrified her so badly many months ago. Yet here and now he was reduced to a pitiful wreck who needed her help simply to move. He had done nothing wrong to her in a long time unless one counted the occasional stupid comment or general rudeness.

Hyde growled, "Okay, good. Show me."

She wheeled him into the cargo hold, where a crate awaited in the middle of the deck. She opened it, stood aside, and let Hyde see it before she bothered to say anything. "There. What do you think?"

He stared at the items within the container. His jaw dropped open, and his eyes bulged out. Nasreen realized he was trying to be certain of what he was looking at before he leapt to conclusions. He did not want to make the mistake of thinking it was something else and have to live with the crushing disappointment.

"You," he muttered and paused as he searched for the right words. "You came through. You did what you said you would...for me. I don't deserve you."

Nasreen had to admit it was the nicest thing he had ever said. "Yes, we always keep our promises, and we did our best. It's not as incredibly advanced and, erm, *overclocked* as your old one was. It's still of high quality and a definite improvement over the current getup, I would say."

Hyde put his one crude mechanical hand on the chair, shifted his weight, clumsily rose from his seat, and wobbled closer to the crate. His legs barely functioned, but he could walk after all.

Nasreen moved closer. "Do you need help?"

"No," he snapped in a raspy, impatient voice. He was too excited by what lay before him. "You did enough. I can handle assembling all this stuff. It's not too different from my old one. Let's start with..."

He pulled out a complete and fully functional cybernetic arm. Like the rest of the suit, it was a sleeker, more modern, and economical build than his old one. The new one was almost completely electronic and powered by advanced, rechargeable batteries.

Hyde's appellation was a shortened form of "Mr. Hydraulic," given the fluid-powered nature of his previous body. Some wise-cracker had come up with "Hyde," referring to the man's well-earned reputation as a killer.

That reputation had begun to fade around the same time he'd lost the hydraulic suit—a unique and terrible wonder of modern technology—forcing him to settle for the crude, barely-tolerable metal skeleton he had used this past year.

Nasreen doubted he could single-handedly reassemble the entire suit, but he seemed earnest about it. Time was wasting. She wanted to get airborne again and begin the search for Ambrose.

She shrugged. "Okay, well, I'll leave you to it. The toolbox at the far corner of the crate might be useful. Let me know if you need help. I'm going to take us into the sky. We're going to retrace Ambrose's flight plan and see what the hell happened to him. He's late."

"Of course, he is," Hyde muttered, but a note of real concern underlaid his gruff façade. "It happens when we have about half the people we need to deal with all the shit lately. Ha! There." He gave the arm another hard *smack,* and something *clicked.* After fiddling with a wire or two and rotating his shoulder, the arm moved. It extended and flexed its elbow, inscribed a circle in the air, and the hand opened to spread its fingers before closing into a fist.

Nasreen nodded. It was good to see the suit was working so far after all the money they'd spent on it. Having Hyde battle-ready by the time they landed might be more than a little useful, the way things had been going.

CHAPTER TEN

The afternoon was waning by the time Dante emerged from the spa. He'd been there a full hour longer than he had estimated or anticipated, even after accounting for Singh's desire to hang around and chat.

Shrugging into his jacket and inhaling the air as he stepped outside, he muttered, "Still enough time. Plenty of time. These people don't sleep much, anyway."

Arms dealers, specifically.

An approaching matron looked at him with a weird expression. Her hearing must have been keen to have picked up on what he said, but he ignored her. Or perhaps it was another instance of someone vaguely recognizing his face from his days as a streamer but not wanting to leap to the conclusion that they'd bumped into a celebrity.

Another wave of relaxed satisfaction went through him as he moved past her, and he nearly paused to breathe out and enjoy it for a moment. He wanted to, but time was fleeting, so he didn't.

It was the massage. Singh had insisted on it, and despite Dante's misgivings, he had agreed. He wanted to keep Singh happy long enough to get the information he needed out of the man. There had also been an element of morbid curiosity. He'd assumed that massages were either pointless, decadent, or in a few disreputable cases, simply a euphemism for certain other, probably illegal activities.

When the whole thing had started, with him and Singh each lying next to each other on two nearby tables, facedown and covered with a towel, he'd felt stupid and awkward about it. Once the masseuses had arrived and started their work, his tension drained away, and surprisingly, he *enjoyed* the whole thing.

Not that he planned to admit it to anyone else for the foreseeable future. He was Dante Shale—he had a reputation to maintain. If people thought he was going soft and pampered on them, he would have an increasingly difficult time getting them to cooperate when he needed information, fast and direct. They would think he was a pushover or given to long flowery conversations.

Shaking his head to clear it of such thoughts, Dante pressed on toward a mostly empty park not far from the spa. It would give him enough privacy to set up the meeting with his contacts. At the same time, it was hardly a suspicious location for a person to linger and check things on their sphere. He would not have much to worry about if someone else stumbled onto him.

As the park drew closer, he recalled the other thing Singh had mentioned. It was the most useful and relevant bit of intel he'd received aside from the short list of names. Specifically, the man had divulged all he knew about retractable carbon filament blades.

There had been a buzz in the circles of people who used or dealt with weapons. Their concealable nature made them a true horror to whoever might end up on the wrong end of them. The blade proper could be hidden within many sorts of devices and deployed with the press of a button or other small trigger or simple action.

Even more interesting was that the hand-weapon blades were incredibly sharp. They could cut through or puncture thinner shuttle bulkheads and possibly city domes, leading to depressurization.

That fact, more than anything, was why they fell into the legal gray area and public opinion was largely against their use. Not to mention the horror inherent in something so unobtrusive that could decapitate multiple people with a single swing.

Most arms dealers wanted nothing to do with the things. It was easier to conduct what was considered shady or dangerous business without giving the authorities extra reasons to investigate them. Some didn't mind the notoriety—those same individuals whose names appeared on Singh's little list.

One specific vendor wasn't shy about touting her stock of carbon filament knives, batons, hatchets, and cane-swords. There was no reason for her to be coy. She had so many outstanding violations, warrants, subpoenas, and past convictions that it would be pointless for her to play nice at the present stage in her career.

Singh had declared, "She calls herself Kali. Evocative, is it not? Perhaps more so for someone from my culture, even though I am a Sikh."

As Singh chuckled, Dante mentioned, "I've heard of Kali. The goddess, I mean. This is the first I've heard of, you know, this particular woman."

"Yes, yes." Singh had lowered his voice. "She is truly something. She touches things that I would not even *look at*. She is willing to sell items that are *worse* than these blades you speak of, and she values her privacy and that of her clients.

"She has no legitimate storefront, no mainstream respectable front business, at least so far. All her transactions are backroom affairs, under the table, conducted with untraceable currency.

"If you go to her for a carbon-blade, she will be accommodating once satisfied that you are not with the police. If you go to her for *information,* well, that may make her highly suspicious. Do not expect her to be charitable or to have much sympathy for your goals, Mr. Shale."

Dante had grimaced into the distance. "Yeah. I'm used to it by now."

Within the park, he went to a tree not far from a bench, leaned against it, and checked his sphere. There was a message from Nasreen, terse but informative. She was still Dirtside. Finding Hyde and Ambrose would be more of a chore than hoped, and she was unsure how long it would take.

"Damn," Dante mumbled. "Well, all the more reason to deal with my little errand while she's busy."

He pulled up a couple of contacts named by Singh—people who had past dealings with Kali but whom Dante had also dealt with. Ideally, they could act as intermediaries who could vouch for his trustworthiness and help set up a meeting with the elusive weapons vendor. He sent messages to them, stating his requests in plain and forthright language, as was his custom.

Midas spoke up. *"Sir, I am collating information about this Kali individual and will be able to report the main findings to you shortly. I've also found some reports about the people killed or injured during our misadventure at the communications relay. I believe I've made an important connection or two."*

Dante put his sphere away and settled on the bench, feigning relaxation like a man on break from his job. A few people filed past, and a young couple stood around chatting not far from him, but no one was paying him too much attention.

"Okay," he said in a low voice. "Tell me."

"I do not have information on everyone involved yet, but a handful of the dead, wounded, or arrested were members of an outfit calling itself Block 9X. They are in essence a mercenary corporation. They also do 'private security.' They are known for hiring 'reformed' criminals and have managed to stay in business despite a somewhat shaky record with the law."

Dante noticed that Midas's personality and awareness had developed to the point that he could hear the sarcastic quotation marks in certain things the AI said. "Interesting. What else?"

Dante watched as the young couple moved closer and kept going, exiting the park on the opposite side.

Within his head, Midas went on. *"Block 9X was named in another violation that also involved Ms. Kali. She provided them with modified sling-guns that resemble advanced miniature crossbows. If you're unfamiliar with them, they can hurl a soft metal, rubber, or plastic slug at a high enough velocity to seriously incapacitate a human. A shot to the temple or throat will kill them.*

"They are not supposed to be powerful enough to penetrate bulkheads and the like. The custom guns produced by Kali were scaled up to the point that they could puncture most body armor and some forms of tempered glass. This resulted in a near-breach of the Pentapolis dome during a shootout between Block 9X and a group of their rivals."

Dante whistled. "Good work, Midas. This is the kind of shit I want to know." He had not heard of Block 9X, but he'd dealt with outfits like them. Hired thugs, for the most part, but not as brutal as Reapers since they mostly operated in the Stations rather than Dirtside. That only meant they had to refine their methods more.

It sounded like Kali was the sort of person who'd be willing to help such people push the limits in pursuit of their goals.

He had goals and was curious how far he could push *her* limits.

Not too surprisingly, Kali insisted on meeting in a foreclosed building that was officially uninhabited according to city records. It lay in a depressed, industrial portion of town, not far from residential and business districts. In this location, they hid in plain sight and had a fair amount of privacy.

When Dante entered the building via an unlocked side door,

two bodyguards immediately accosted him. One was big, and the other was more his size, average but noticeably spry and sinewy. They wore dark glasses and long coats. Given that they worked for an arms dealer, he could guarantee that each had a veritable arsenal of small but effective concealed weapons, both lethal and nonlethal.

"Hold it." The big guy stepped in front of him. The other, smaller man circled to Dante's flank, where he could intercept him if he tried to dodge his larger partner in either direction.

Dante flashed a brief, humorless smile. "Hi. I'm Dante Shale. I have an appointment, and Zhu Wen vouched for me. I have a knife under my jacket on my right side, but that's it."

The smaller guy chuckled. "Oh, smart guy, huh? You think you know how this is going to play out, that all you have to do is act like you know the whole procedure and we'll be impressed at how fuckin' smart you are. Well, that's *not* how it works. You stand there while we frisk you and keep your mouth shut, and if you can do *that* without pissing us off or doing anything stupid, Kali will think about letting you in."

That was what Dante had expected. "Okay." He put his arms up. The smaller guy suddenly produced a dart launcher, likely of the poisonous variety, and held it aimed at Dante's throat while the big guy patted him down. When he found the knife, he took it.

"You'll get it back," the man rumbled. "Once Kali says you can go."

Dante didn't complain. He did pay attention to where the man stashed the blade on his body.

They led him across the floor of the darkened lobby to a short hallway, opened a door, and motioned him inside. Once he crossed the threshold, the smaller guy stepped in after him and positioned himself in Dante's blind spot, with a direct line to his kidney. His hulking partner stayed in the hallway, blocking it off.

Before him was a small, spare office. Another bodyguard,

more medium-sized but thick with muscle, stood to the side of the desk in the center. Behind the desk sat a short, wiry woman with wide, round staring eyes wearing a heavy overcoat and a red scarf. She'd bundled her black hair atop her head and had a long scar running down her cheek.

"Dante Shale," she intoned in a soft but raspy voice. "You look familiar. From your streams, I mean. Ha. Why haven't I heard anything about you for months now? Who do you work for now? I would be most curious to know."

Dante's eyes drifted, for a second, over her shoulder to a wheelable heavy backpack resting in the rear corner of the room, likely containing merchandise samples. Then he looked back at the woman.

"Myself. My partner and I are still in the same business, but we don't stream anymore. We work for whoever our current clients are. We're not anyone's employees. You can look us up at—"

She cut him off with an abrupt slashing motion. He tensed since it almost looked like she was about to draw a weapon, but he did not otherwise react. He only kept an eye on her.

"I don't care." She stood, pushing the chair back. "What is it you want? Zhu Wen said something about retractable carbon blades. I may have heard of such things." She smirked. They both knew that at least one of the things was in the pack in the corner. She was going through the charade of plausible deniability to be safe.

Dante looked into her eyes with a neutral yet intense expression. He usually gave people that look when he wanted to cut the bullshit without being too abrasive. Yet.

"Have you heard of Block 9X?" He paused. "I'm here because I want to know more about them and their operations. It doesn't have anything to do with you or with carbon blades. I can pay you for your time. You may still consider me a customer."

She exchanged a glance with the short guy, who still hovered behind Dante and out of his field of vision. Dante felt him inching closer.

Kali snapped, "I am not a snitch or informant, and I do not sell information. You are wasting my time if that is what you expect. Either you want to buy something from me, or—"

"I want to buy a carbon-blade, after all," he interjected. "Only one. A personal defense tool. I was impressed at the way the Block 9X guys handled those things. I ran into them pretending to be security for a hacked public communications relay in Atlantica Metro. Don't security forces usually stick to less lethal weapons? Makes me wonder if those carbon blades are as scary as people say they are."

Kali snorted. "You are trying to manipulate me into blurting something out. Hah! I see these tactics all the time from under-cover cops. That is what you are, isn't it? Better job security, now that you are no longer a popular celebrity?

"Or if you do not work for the police, one of your clients has hired you to spy on my other customers and me. I have enough problems without rumors that I sell out some clients to others. Plenty of people want my head on a plate. I only sell weapons. Get out!"

She flourished her hand toward the door and glared at him.

"No. I already told you that I'm not working for the cops. I'm not doing industrial espionage or anything either. My friends and I had a little personal problem recently, and I want to know what they might have to do with it. I'd be happy to talk to them about it directly. All I need from you is—"

Kali blinked in an oddly conspicuous way.

Dante's instincts kicked in. He stepped sharply to the side, and a poison dart from behind whisked past him, grazing his coat before embedding itself in the desk. Then all hell broke loose as the small guy behind him and the muscleman beside the desk attacked at once.

Dante grabbed the corner of the desk and flipped it over,

causing Kali to backpedal away from it, blocking the muscle-bound guy's attack and driving the desk's opposite corner into his thighs. Then he spun to deal with the small man who'd emptied his dart launcher.

"You fuck!" the little guy snarled. "You stupid fuck." He lunged toward the Marauder with a weird underhand punch.

He had a wrist knife and was going to stab Dante in the leg or groin. Dante clawed his eyes with one hand while knocking his wrist down with the other. The blade flicked out but missed his thigh by a hand's breadth.

The little guy was fast but too emotional. He was the type who liked to win a fight in the first move and became enraged if it stretched on any longer than that. He was already descending into a frenzy, jeering and flailing his knife around. He was skilled but undisciplined.

Dante took a grazing blow to the arm that drew blood but didn't do any serious damage. He stepped forward and elbowed the man in the face. It knocked his head back and took him off-balance. The ripped guy was advancing around the desk.

Dante picked up the little man and threw him. He crashed into the muscleman, and both fell in a thrashing tangle of limbs.

Then he pivoted as the last guard, the big one, rushed into the room with an ashen-faced expression of grim urgency. Kali slowly backed away from the fight toward her precious merchan-dise pack.

One of the drawers was sticking out of the desk. Dante seized it, ripped it free, and hurled it at the onrushing giant. The man failed to expect any such move and froze. It broke apart against his arms when he tried to deflect it, but the shards scratched his face and obscured his vision.

It was enough of a delay for Dante to swoop in, go low, and punch the man hard in the testicles. He was wearing a cup, but not a very high-quality one, and it crunched under the blow. A shudder went through the man. Dante rolled between his legs and pulled his knife free from the man's belt.

By the time the guard turned, Dante had drawn the blade. He plunged it through the man's bicep, twisted it, and as the guard groaned in agony, Dante grabbed his neck and slammed his head into the wall. He crumpled, and Dante pulled the knife free from his bleeding arm.

He spun. The little guy was down for the count, thanks to the elbow to the face and the impact of being tossed. The muscled guy was back on his feet and had pulled a knife. He stayed in place, seeming unenthusiastic about fighting the Marauder to the death.

Kali took advantage of the little pause. One of her dark, bony hands disappeared into her jacket, and she pulled out a handgun in a flash.

Dante's eyes fixed on it, and he froze. He wasn't sure if he was shocked or not. The woman held a huge, old-fashioned revolver made of stainless steel with a five- or six-inch barrel. The cylinder held live shells, and the barrel's bore was wide enough that it had to be at least a .44. Although antiquated, it was a weapon that would turn his head into a fruit salad quite handily.

It was also incredibly illegal. Traditional and pulsecore firearms were universally verboten on the Stations due to the danger they posed to the structural integrity of the domes. Not that Kali seemed like the sort of person who cared much about legality.

She hissed, "Dante Shale, you are making me dislike you. I don't think I want to deal with you ever again."

Dante inhaled through his nose and kept his eyes focused on her. He was dimly aware of the knife-wielding bodyguard at her side, enough to keep track of the man's movements.

"Guns like that have a lot of recoil and can be difficult to shoot accurately," he pointed out. "Either you can tell me what I want to know about Block 9X and we can part amicably, notwithstanding this little scuffle." He paused.

"Or you can shoot me and hope I die instantly from the first shot because if not, you will finally have made me *angry*. Then I will use whatever life I have left to beat the information out of you."

For a split second, her eyes reminded him of an animal about to bite. For all his fortitude, his heart fluttered. Her finger put a little extra pressure on the trigger.

Then it passed. The woman's face relaxed, and she burst out laughing. She lowered the gun so it pointed at his legs rather than his head and eased her finger off the trigger.

"I like you. You are every bit as crazy as they say. The *cold* kind of crazy that is. It would be better not to become enemies or leave dead bodies here. I think I will give you this information..."

The way she inflected the last sentence, he knew more was coming. He waited, still staring her down.

"On one condition."

He sighed. "Figures. What is it?"

CHAPTER ELEVEN

Hyde bellowed, *"Hey! Watch it,* for fuck's sake!"

Nasreen was focused on the shuttle's controls and could not be bothered to look back at him. He was still his old, charming self, and she could not shake the suspicion that her charitable gift of a new body was reinflating his ego.

"I *am* watching it, Hyde. We hit a patch of rough weather, and I'm doing my best to keep us steady." Her hands worked through a steady roster of activity, steering and tapping buttons and gauges, moving fast but gently to neutralize the effects of turbulence.

A storm had risen, one more intense than those typical for this region of Earth. Blowing dust and churning clouds of moisture filled the air, and the winds were strong enough to require constant correction.

When she hit a calmer spot, she glanced back at her passenger. She wanted to check how he was doing.

Hyde had finished reassembling himself from the components she'd brought. No longer the shambling, half-destroyed wreck he had been since his devastation on Pentapolis, he nonetheless cut quite a different figure from how he'd been before *that*.

His original suit had given him the appearance of a huge and terrible steel ogre, bulky and irregular enough that it belied how fast and coordinated he was despite the jerky nature of his movements. His unnatural-looking red hair and beard, deep gruff voice, and propensity for violence heightened the impression.

His new body was average, to the extent that an oversized cyborg form could be "average." On its surface, it resembled a standard male human body coated in form-fitting armor, sleek and pearly, almost ceramic. Its mechanical aspects stayed largely hidden. It also made Hyde smaller than he had been overall. Still, he was taller and heavier than the great majority of people.

He needed time to adjust to it. He could not overcome a year of making do with the cheap and clanky substitute they'd stitched together for him in an instant. At least he could move his limbs in the right direction and mostly keep his balance.

Nasreen hoped he would be in a proper state to rappel off the ship and grab their mutual friend when the time came.

"I'm getting a better feel for this thing." He echoed her thoughts.

Nasreen exhaled and returned her attention to the displays attached to the shuttle's external camera system. Then her heart leapt, skipping a beat in the process, and her attention and focus sharpened totally on one point.

"There." She pointed at the viewscreen out of habit, although Hyde probably couldn't see from where he was. "I spotted Ambrose's shuttle. Dammit. He went down in a valley. I don't see any smoke, so that's a good sign, but it doesn't look like he stopped for a break."

It was possible that there *was* smoke and she hadn't been able to discern it amid the storm's effects.

Hyde's feet *clanked* as he struggled to move closer to the cockpit. "So, what, he managed to crash? Into what? He usually flies well above the hilltops."

It was amazing that a man far older than most humans thanks to his many augmentations could be so ignorant of certain things, Nasreen reflected. People who had never tried to fly sometimes were.

"Well, if it wasn't the weather, it was probably an internal problem with the ship. You said parts and resources were always a problem. Something might have failed or broken down, and he had to attempt an emergency landing. Or maybe a health issue overtook him. I don't know. Either way, we're going into that valley to recover him. I hope he's okay."

Hyde asked, "We? Both of us?"

"If necessary. It would be better for me to stay with the ship and you be the one to find and grab him now that you have a new suit or body. Whatever. You'll have a lot more strength. I'll assist if needed."

He shrugged, and his new shoulders whirred faintly. "Okay, fine. You're not the one who was on the verge of getting your ass kicked all day. This little ride is the first break I've had in a good twenty hours."

"Let's get this done quickly and efficiently, and once Ambrose is on board, I should be able to handle everything else," she retorted. "I'll get us back home, and you can get some rest."

Deep within she had doubts about how feasible that would be. It was disturbingly uncommon for any rescue operation, especially when Dirtside, to be quick or efficient. Dante had taught her to always assume that complications would arise, to expect the unexpected, and be ready to adapt and re-adapt to anything.

The thought had crossed her mind when the external microphone picked up what sounded like a crackling series of gunshots.

She added, "Hyde, someone might be shooting out there. Be careful. I'll get you as close to Ambrose's shuttle as I can in this turbulence. If he's, um, conscious, he's smart enough to know to stay with the ship."

The giant cyborg tottered toward the door and hooked a zip line to himself. His mechanical movements were still awkward but noticeably smoother than they had been minutes before. "Great!" he bellowed. "This is what we needed to make sure we're all having fun. If someone's shooting, it means someone's alive."

It was true. Nasreen took some heart.

She brought them into the valley, slowing down and going into a higher-level hover pattern. Thankfully, some of the storm distortion was clearing now that the surrounding hills blocked part of the wind, dust, and vapor.

Ambrose's shuttle came closer into view. The wreck looked survivable, but she still could not see Ambrose, and the craft was in no condition to fly out. Nasreen's best guess was that the turbulence had knocked him into a protruding cliff or something and forced him to attempt a hasty landing when and where he could.

She steadied the ship. For a normal human to attempt a drop at this elevation would have been extremely dangerous. Hyde was hardly normal, and she had seen him leap from greater heights before. "You ready?"

"Sure." He fiddled with the zip line. "Hold on a second. If I lose another limb, it's your money wasted, not mine." Then he checked a pulsecore rifle he had grabbed from the armory and tapped the mic on his headset.

Nasreen opened the bay door.

Something crashed into the shuttle and rocked them hard to one side. The impact tossed her halfway out of her seat and set half a dozen alarms on the console blaring and flashing.

"Oh, shit!" She grasped the chair and console, barely held in place by her seatbelt. "Hyde!"

A growling sound from the cyborg turned into a deep, echoing wail as the man plummeted into the void, thrown prematurely by whatever had hit the ship. A second or two after he vanished, the zip line, sans him, snapped back into sight. The violent motion had thrown him out before he could get it fastened properly, leaving him untethered.

Nasreen righted herself and seized the steering components in time to veer aside from a looming cliff wall. The shuttle spiraled around the valley's circumference as it descended at twice the speed any sane pilot would have recommended. She tried to slow it down, knowing it would be impossible to get airborne again before the ground rose to claim her. She would have to attempt the same thing Ambrose had.

"Here goes." Her jaw clenched as she aimed for a relatively flat patch of land covered with bushes and bracken.

The automatic buffer system used hover tech to partially repel impacts and minimize damage. It kicked in, preventing the shuttle from scraping half of itself off on the ground. It rocked the craft badly and required more correction from the pilot. Nasreen was struggling to stay in her seat. The way ahead of her was clear of major obstacles. She kept pulling back on speed and seeking the path of least resistance, and friction brought her to a grinding halt not far from a stand of trees.

She remembered to breathe. Everything was still and silent for the moment. She checked the various viewscreens. Only one of them had failed during her semi-crash, quasi-landing.

Something caught her attention at once. A detail that did not belong and stood out from the expected landscape. A pile of components assembled into a machine, resting on a low ridge halfway up one of the hills on the valley's rim, with two human figures squatting next to it.

It took her a couple of seconds to determine what it was—a crude but effective catapult or ballista. The hostile Dirtwalkers of the region had loaded it with pieces of scrap from nearby ruins or chunks of rock from the land.

She drew in her breath with a hissing sound, tore off her seatbelt, and headed for the armory before she did anything else. "Goddammit. They knocked us out of the sky. *That* was what brought Ambrose down."

Above and around her, the winds howled. The storm was less severe down here, but the valley still was getting part of it.

Nasreen grabbed a short-barreled rifle with conventional ammo. The prospect of getting pummeled by chunks of the hills had induced a sudden paranoia about avalanches. Better not to go with a pulsecore or anything else with explosive properties.

Then she tried to raise Hyde on her suit's comms system. "Hyde. This is Nasreen. Are you there? Are you okay? Over."

Nothing. He might have been out of sorts, or the crash could have damaged his radio equipment.

Or perhaps the fall's distance, unaided by the zip line, had been too much even for his augmented frame. Maybe Nasreen's shuttle had landed atop him or crashed into him during her desperate landing.

Cursing everything that had happened since she'd arrived on Earth, she strode to the door, rifle at low ready and prepared—as Dante would have put it—to adapt to the situation.

As soon as she was clear of the ship, Nasreen made for the closest thing approximating cover, a gentle rise in the land with a couple of thick bushes growing from it. The two Dirtwalkers operating the catapult were unlikely to be the only ones present, and her dramatic landing had not made a secret of her arrival.

Someone shot at her. She ducked and half-rolled toward the depression behind the hillock with the two bushes, scanning everything around her. A form moved on a slope in the hills about a hundred and ten yards out.

She raised her rifle, unable to get a bead on the tribesman but had ascertained his position well enough to fire two shots that would probably drive him to cover for a moment. The report of her gun echoed through the vale, piercing through the storm's ambient noise.

A volley of shots rang out, mostly lead-based guns from the sound of it. Pulsecores made a distinctive *thunk-burst* noise when fired, noticeably different from the miniature thunderclaps of conventional firearms.

Nasreen hugged the ground. Most of the shots had come from the catapult's direction, but at least one or two came from the opposite way. Part of the bush above her shattered under the impact of a bullet, and she realized it had been the latter shooter who'd done it.

Her head moved in that direction. She could faintly see the top of Ambrose's crashed shuttle.

"Ambrose!" she shouted, at the risk of exposing her position. "It's me, Nasreen!"

Two more shots went high of her.

A familiar voice called, "Nasreen? Dammit, they shot you down as well. My ship can't fly. I don't know how many of them there are. Is Hyde here?"

The Dirtwalkers took three or four more potshots before Nasreen could answer.

"I don't know. He came with me, but he fell out when we got hit. I can't raise him on comms. Work your way toward me. Can you walk? I'll meet you halfway. Pretty sure my shuttle is still functional. I'll cover you."

She aimed toward the foothills, firing four shots toward the general area where their foes had gathered. She could not see anyone to hit them, but the idea was to pin them down while Ambrose moved. She tried to aim high to decrease the chance of accidentally hitting Hyde if by some chance he was still around. His armor was mostly bulletproof, but a stray round to the face would still be bad.

Fortunately, Ambrose was not wounded badly enough to impair his mobility, and she saw him struggling toward her through the bracken. When he paused to shoot back amid the sporadic pops of the Dirtwalkers' gunfire, she half-crawled, half-dashed toward him, keeping as low as she could.

It sounded like the tribespeople were getting closer. Above them, the pair manning the catapult were loading a boulder into it.

Nasreen suddenly shook with fury. "Oh no you don't." She aimed, released her breath, and fired a single shot. One of the Dirtwalkers spun and fell, bleeding onto the device, and the other ran out of sight. The catapult stood useless for now with the boulder resting beside it.

As Ambrose approached, he implored, "We need to get out of here. There are more of them than you think, and they're moving in. They're either the same tribe raiding us or one of their allies. They don't take prisoners."

Nasreen wondered if that was a good thing since prisoners in violent societies sometimes wished their enemies *had* killed them in battle.

"Yes, we need to get to my shuttle. As long as we can avoid that catapult, they won't be able to shoot us down with rifles. I want to find Hyde. We can't abandon him."

The two crawled toward one another, finally stopping about fifteen feet apart. Then the whole mass of shrubs, weeds, and small dead trees rustled as at least a dozen men rushed through it, springing out of ambush and shouldering their guns.

Nasreen's rifle came up in a flash, and she emptied the rest of her magazine, spraying lead toward the war band with little thought of picking individual targets. At least two of the attackers fell dead, but the rest melted back into the landscape.

She ejected the empty mag and felt her jacket for more. She had brought only one spare and cursed herself for it. Dante would have been furious with her for not expecting stiffer resistance.

Ambrose stumbled toward her and took another clumsy shot toward the field as she reloaded. He was using an old assault rifle from the early twenty-first century. It was a decent weapon but typical of the hand-me-downs expected for someone living on Earth. He limped. Something had happened to his leg or ankle, but not serious enough to cripple him.

Nasreen beckoned. "Come on. I don't have much ammo left."

"I am almost out," Ambrose lamented. She'd always thought him a rather whiny individual, but right now she couldn't blame him for it.

Then half a dozen more Dirtwalkers crested the low hillock, their sallow faces livid with cold rage. One fired his weapon instantly. Nasreen's fast reflexes kicked in, but the bullet still grazed the armor plate on her bicep. She shot back but missed.

The others were ready to kill.

Hyde suddenly burst free from the bushes he had been crouching behind. Whether wounded, hiding, or dazed, he decided to stand and walk out.

"Fuck this shit!" he roared, striding directly toward the advancing mass of tribesmen. Clenched in the metal fingers of his right hand was what remained of his rifle. The end of the barrel had broken off, and part of the chassis had cracked into oblivion. He gripped it around the warped middle and hoisted it over his shoulder, waving the stock like the head of a club.

Only one of the Dirtwalkers got a shot off before he plowed into them. The bullet struck the curved and hardened plate over what would have been his right pectoral, denting it but deflecting off. Hyde ignored it.

Then he brought the rifle down mace-like on the head of the man who'd shot him. The Dirtwalker tried to spring to his feet and retreat, but the stock caught him in the back of the skull, crunching it and sending him sprawling.

Another charged and aimed, trying to fire the gun point-blank at Hyde's face, but the cyborg swatted the barrel aside with his free hand and punched the man in the chest, collapsing his ribcage and driving him back to spit up blood as he fell.

As Hyde roared again and swung his makeshift club in a broad circle, the tribespeople's resolve broke. They scattered in two directions, splitting into two groups and seeking to get away before the battle, now lost, could claim their lives.

"Ha, ha!" Hyde guffawed while striding closer to Nasreen and Ambrose. "They look like they're going to regroup and try something else unless we get the hell out of here."

Nasreen nodded. "I agree. Back to my shuttle. Ambrose, we'll have to leave yours. It's too badly damaged—and not worth your life."

Ambrose groaned. His mind was already turning over the consequences of losing his ship, but he offered no argument to the part about saving his skin.

While Hyde covered them with his metal body, the two unmodified humans rushed toward the opened bay door of Nasreen's craft, ducking around obstacles and clearing the ramp as the Dirtwalkers began taking potshots again. Hyde came in after them, and Nasreen rushed to close the door.

"No catapult operators anymore, and they're not getting through the hull of this thing with only small arms fire," she pointed out.

As the door shut she dashed to the cockpit, dragging Ambrose behind her. He did not want to do much of anything, but as long as he was conscious, she might as well make use of him.

"Am, you're going to be my copilot. It will be nice to have someone on board who understands how difficult flying can be."

Hyde grumbled, "I heard that."

Nasreen flashed him a tight smile. "I'm sure you did. By the way, thanks for saving our lives."

CHAPTER TWELVE

Dante sighed. It was more of a breathy, raspy groan—the sound a man makes when he knows he has to do something but is not looking forward to it. He reached into the trunk compartment and picked up the two massive gun cases, which seemed even heavier now than when he'd first put them into the rented shuttle car.

Carrying them was well within his physical abilities, although it wasn't much fun. What bothered him was that he hadn't wanted the damn things, but he had his reputation and principles to consider. He never broke a deal.

Nasreen's shuttle had been idling in hover mode as he pulled up, and as he started across the floor of the small vehicle bay they had acquired, she stepped out the side door to greet him. So far, no one else had come out with her.

"Well, hello there." She spoke in a low but clear voice. "What are those? Also, you will be happy to hear that my end of the mission was a success."

He closed his eyes for a second and nodded. "Good. Are they with you now? I'll show you what they are in a minute. I have the info I was looking for, which is much more important than these goddamn things."

Ambrose slid out behind Nasreen. He looked tired, half-confused, and ambivalent, but that was hardly uncommon. Life Dirtside had changed him. He was thinner and harder-looking. "Hello, Dante."

"Hi, Am." He kept walking toward the shuttle, wondering if either of them would offer to take the heavy cases. "Glad you could make it. As usual, we're not asking you for help because of how *good* things have been lately."

The pilot's face crinkled, his mouth a sour grimace, his eyes calm with resignation. "Yes, Nasreen told me about it. I would have expected nothing else."

Then a third figure emerged. He was taller than the others by a head and gleamed with new armor. A faint electronic whirring accompanied all his movements. The dour expression beneath his red beard turned into a wolfish grin.

"Dante! What are those, guns? Here, let me see." He stomped forward, pushing Ambrose aside. Dante flashed back to what Hyde was like in his original bodysuit. A veritable monstrosity. Now he was less overtly frightening but in some ways more impressive. The new suit had an elegant simplicity, an economy of form and function.

Dante raised the cases. "Don't open them or run off with them. Yeah, thanks."

Hyde snatched them up, jostling each in his hand to guess its contents, and carried them easily. "Not many guns. I was hoping for more."

"We have enough. More than we need, thanks to my having to buy those things. Kali insisted on it."

Ambrose blinked. "Who?"

Dante flexed a hand, pleased to have them free again. "It's a long story. Arms dealer I found through my old contacts who gave me some leads on the people we're looking for. I had to kick the shit out of her bodyguards, so to smooth things over, she insisted I buy some off-market goods from her as collateral." He frowned. "To ensure I don't rat on her if the authorities became involved, she demanded that I break the law myself. I said yes."

Hyde laughed in his low, grinding, unpleasant way. "That's fair."

Nasreen's eyes were hooded. She did not look pleased. "I don't like the idea, but with our apprentices held God-knows-where and some other faction trying to kill us, I won't say you made the wrong choice. Let's get into the back room before we continue this discussion."

Once they were safely out of the main bay area and sequestered in the privacy of rear storage, Hyde put the cases down and opened them before Dante could give him permission. If he was so excited, it was better to view the contents and get it over with.

The cyborg looked at the objects within. "What the hell are these things? Guns, obviously. Never seen their like before, though."

Dante nodded. "Most people haven't. They're prototype smart rifles. Not even on the market yet. They're still experimental. When they do come out, the contract is only for government types. So yes, these are *very* illegal. I shouldn't have to remind anyone to keep your mouths shut about them."

Hyde's mouth was hanging open in awe. "Heh, heh. For something like this, I can keep quiet if I have to. What do they do? What's so 'smart' about them?"

Nasreen chimed in, "I've heard a thing or two about the program to develop those. Essentially they shoot homing bullets and can switch between different ammo types with the press of a button. That's the goal, anyway."

"Yeah," Dante confirmed. "Again, I don't fucking know how functional these things are. If they work the way they're supposed to, we can electronically pin the bullets to a target, and the smart ammo has some mid-flight self-correcting capabilities. Not to the point of looping in circles, but it can adjust its trajectory to follow the target up to about a forty-five-degree angle."

Ambrose whistled. "That sounds dangerous for anyone standing in front of the thing when fired. A fleeing target could draw many bullets after him and into innocent bystanders, maybe."

Nasreen pointed out, "That is exactly why they're putting them through so much testing, I'd wager."

Dante nodded. "Not a weapon for every situation, but if they work, they could be damn good in *some* cases. Also, the ammo-switching. It comes with dual magazines, which is part of why they're so heavy.

"They can switch between hard shot intended for full-on combat like you'd see Dirtside or soft frangible rounds that still pack a punch against also-soft targets but are a lot safer when it comes to overpenetration or damaging machinery. We could probably use those inside the Stations. Not much danger of breaching the domes."

Hyde chortled. "The eggheads never fail to impress me when it comes to inventing new ways to kill people. How did this Kali person get hold of these, anyway?"

Dante had wandered toward the door to peek out and ensure that no one suspicious might have been drifting closer to their abode. "I have no idea. She specializes in getting things that no one is supposed to have. She's the type who doesn't care how illegal it is since she already has a two-mile-long rap sheet."

"I like her already," Hyde mused.

Nasreen stepped forward. "Well, maybe we can arrange a date between you two later. First we need to rescue Jolo, Braelin, and Mugoi. Dante, what did you find? Ambrose, are you going to stick with us and not do anything stupid?"

Dante waited while Ambrose moaned with a miserable

droopy look. "Yes, don't worry. I will do what I must and head back Dirtside when it's over. That is all. If I were to betray you again, I suppose you would be justified in finally killing me."

Dante nodded. "Correct. I'd rather not, so I'm glad you don't plan to make me."

Hyde picked up the guns and examined them with giddy, childlike joy. For all his faults, Dante at least trusted the brute of a man not to fire one indoors. Dante motioned Nasreen to come closer as he related all he'd learned to her.

"I'm almost positive the group that came after me with the carbon blades is called Block 9X. I'm not sure if they're the ones who kidnapped our apprentices. Going after them is a start, either way. I know the location of their main operations. Not only the obvious public offices, which are mostly a front anyway but the secret places where they do the real work."

Nasreen arched her brows. "I've heard of them. Security company, hires ex-cons, kind of shady reputation?"

"Yeah." Dante rubbed his eyes and steeled himself. He had decided on a course of action but wasn't sure how Nasreen would feel about it. "Since they don't fuck around, we hit them hard and fast. When the smoke clears, we sort things out with the survivors and let them explain the situation to us to the best of their ability."

Nasreen's mouth fell open. "Umm. Dante. There are a lot of potential problems with openly attacking a mostly legitimate company and using terrorist tactics against them. Especially if their HQ is somewhere in orbit. We *cannot* use the same tactics in the Stations that we would Dirtside."

He had half-expected this. "Tell them the same thing. I'm amazed they're considered even *semi*-legitimate."

Pursing her lips in obvious exasperation, his partner continued. "Listen, instead of blowing a hole through their walls and holding guns to everyone's heads, it might be more effective to get into Block 9X ourselves. We can find out if they're the ones who took our apprentices. If they're not, they might be looking to go after mutual enemies. We could get a lead on the other group by posing as extra muscle and learn more about how Block 9X operates."

Dante stared at her. "Well, that is a good idea. Honestly, you seemed so urgent about everything that I assumed you wanted to do whatever was fastest, regardless of how risky it was."

She shook her head. "Not if there's a major risk of total failure. Our friends are still alive, I think. They can last an extra day or two if it means the difference between freeing them eventually or freeing them never because we got ourselves killed or arrested."

Ambrose gave his two cents. "I am with Nasreen on this, although neither of those plans will be easy. Or fun."

Hyde snapped, "Says who?" He was cradling one of the smart rifles like a puppy.

Dante's eyes wandered. "I don't know. They probably saw me back at the comms relay. It's not like no one ever recognizes my face in public or yours. In some ways, your way might be even riskier."

While Nasreen pondered his words, Ambrose added, "Oh, and if you can disguise yourselves, won't these people be looking for dirty hard-case types like themselves? No offense, I know both of you are tougher than you look."

"Point taken," Nasreen conceded.

There was a moment of silence. Then all three of their gazes went toward the group's fourth member in almost preternatural unison.

Hyde looked at them and coughed. "Well, this suit is kinda *pretty*. Some people know I got busted down to a shell of my past self. I'm not the Reaper of all Reapers that I used to be. Still..."

"Still," Dante echoed. "If I wasn't someone with a ton of combat experience under my belt, I wouldn't mess with you in a dark alley. You'll do."

Nasreen snarked, "You get to intimidate Station-bound civilians for the first time in a year, Mr. Curtidor." No one used his real name often. That, too, might be a benefit.

A wolfish grin spread across Hyde's leering, weather-beaten face. "I like it." He stood straighter. "Time to be a bad guy again."

CHAPTER THIRTEEN

Hyde gloated. "Check this out, *pendejos*. Heh, heh." He pointed at the mass of metal and polymer where his right bicep would have been.

They were standing before the shuttle's bay door, about to disembark and vanish into the throngs of Nuevo Rio. Everyone was suited up and geared up. Rio had a somewhat laxer policy on weapons than many Stations, allowing the carrying of them if they were less lethal or partially disassembled. It resulted from the public outcry over the populace's difficulty defending themselves from rampant crime.

Nasreen peered at his arm. "Oh. A decal? Is that like the equivalent of a tattoo? It looks pretty cool, I guess. Not the same bragging rights of gritting through the pain with having that inked into flesh, now is there?"

Hyde frowned. He seemed legitimately disappointed. "When you replace most of your body with armor and machinery, you're already past having bragging rights about dealing with modifications, *chica*."

Dante looked at the decal. "Flaming skull. Completely unnecessary, but yeah, it might, uh, give the right impression to these people. How did you afford it?"

Midas spoke aloud, his voice chiming through Dante's skull and into the air. "I took care of it out of the discretionary budget, sir. Hyde and I conferred on minor upgrades he could use, and I helped him select and order a few things. I hope you don't mind."

Hyde chortled while Dante scowled. "No more. Maybe later. He has what he needs. Now, let's go."

Ambrose instantly proclaimed from the cockpit, "I will wait with the shuttle! That was part of the plan. Right?"

"Yes, Ambrose," Dante reassured him. "Enjoy your non-participation in the interesting stuff. You're a good pilot, and we need you available for that purpose."

Which included being able to buzz him for an emergency getaway should that become necessary.

Leaving him behind, the other three walked out into the docks, passing through the city's minimal and disinterested security protocol before being released into the streets.

Nuevo Rio was formed from a large portion of Rio de Janeiro that the people of decades past had successfully scooped out of Earth's crust and elevated to the stars. Plus some additions made since the early days of the Station system. It was known for a large degree of cultural diversity even by the standards of large cities, as well as its lively and impressive arts scene.

That was only half of its reputation. The other half was the well-known fact that Rio's leaders struggled to keep a lid on the ever-simmering kettle of corruption and criminality that was the city's core. It was easy to find illegal activity in its lowest and pettiest forms and at the highest levels of social organization.

This made it the perfect place for an outfit like Block 9X to hold their *actual* meetings. As opposed to the fake ones they supposedly held at their official offices on Atlantica Central Station.

The plan called for letting Hyde take the lead. It was one of the many risk elements they had agreed to live with.

"Hey!" Hyde bellowed at some guy who brushed past him roughly. "*Chinga tu madre.* Yeah, you heard me!"

Half of the crowd looked at him, but no one confronted him.

Dante and Nasreen walked in tandem behind the cyborg, close enough to intervene if something went south but far enough back that they could claim not to be with him.

Nasreen whispered, "We *had* to bring the loose cannon who speaks Spanish as his first language into a primarily Spanish-speaking city where people get stabbed daily over verbal slights? Perhaps this wasn't the best idea, after all."

Dante was tempted to say, "I told you so," but he only grunted and shrugged. He was tense and as concerned as she, but over-worrying would accomplish nothing.

Instead, he opined, "He's practicing. Getting into character."

Hyde probably heard them, but he gave no indication of it. He only stomped along through colorful markets, crowded squares, and beside buzzing lanes, heckling random passersby—threats for the men, catcalls for the women. Somehow, they avoided getting into any fights. To his credit Hyde kept his mouth shut when they passed people who looked like serious trouble.

It wasn't that Hyde was afraid of them. Dante doubted the cybernetic ex-Reaper feared many people. For all his abrasiveness and instability, he wasn't such a moron as to provoke a full-scale gang war while they were in the middle of an errand.

Block 9X's HQ was in a squat, dark building in a marginal part of town, surrounded by empty lots and half-operational processing facilities. There was enough commercial activity during the day that it wasn't *too* private and the workers in the area were mostly roughneck types. It was out from under the noses of the authorities, the hoi-polloi, and families with kids.

As they approached the front entrance, Dante spoke sharply. "Remember the script, Hyde. You might have to improvise, but try to stick as close to it as possible." He scratched his fake facial hair. It wasn't much of a disguise even combined with sunglasses, but it was better than nothing.

Hyde grumbled without words and flung open the doors, barging in like he owned the place with Dante and Nasreen covering his flanks.

A man in plainclothes behind a reception desk was chatting with two uniformed security guards. The aesthetic of the place was bare bones but functional. It was more like the waiting room of an auto body shop than the lobby of a doctor or executive.

The three men looked up in unison, their eyes hooded. Dante saw them shift into a heightened state of alertness. No panic, only a cold realization that trouble might be coming. Any time he perceived that trait in others, he was dealing with people he should not underestimate.

Hyde barked, "*Hola!* I'm here to apply for a job. My friends, too. You're hiring, aren't you?"

While the two guards spread out to either side, the receptionist remarked, "Who gave you that idea, big guy?" The accent was vaguely British or perhaps Scandinavian. Like many of the company's employees, he was not from Rio.

"Word on the street," Hyde retorted. "I'm the type of big guy you need. Know how I know that? Because if you don't want to grant me an interview, I could walk through you guys and get one anyway. We don't want to do that, do we? No, it's better to talk like civilized people. Heh, heh."

He grinned evilly. It reminded Dante how much he preferred having the massive Reaper as a friend rather than an enemy.

The guards looked miffed, and their hands slowly moved closer to the shock batons at their belts. Dante guessed that at least one of them probably had a concealed low-power gun.

The leery-eyed receptionist didn't respond directly about an interview. "What's your name? And these other two."

Dante spoke first. "Luciano."

Nasreen added, "Katowice."

Hyde glanced back at them and stretched his arms. "You can call me HDH. That stands for *hombre de hojalata.* You gringo fucks know what that means?"

The security goon on the left smirked. "I am no gringo. It means 'man of tin.' Yes, we can see you have augmentation. That makes us more interested than we would be if you were normal."

A door behind the desk opened. Out strode an overweight and greasy-looking man with an air of legitimate toughness and a scar on his chin. "The fuck is all this commotion? Who are these assholes?" The accent was American, maybe Brooklynite. He was probably from Pentapolis.

Facing the man down as the guards hesitated, the trio repeated their names, and Hyde repeated his request.

The oily man snorted. "We ain't hiring. Get lost."

"Bullshit!" Hyde roared, taking a step forward. The guards fell into fighting stances with their hands on their weapons, but they waited. Hyde went on, "Everyone knows the score with you guys. You need extra muscle. I have *plenty.* Give me an interview. It will make everyone happy, I promise."

The heavyset man exchanged glances with the guards, then looked at the cyborg. "In back. Don't try anything. I never said you're hired. Only that I'm willing to talk to you for two or three minutes. All three of you."

Dante and Nasreen nodded and followed as Hyde *clanked* after the man, passing through the doorway. One of the guards followed them into the hall.

Beyond the corridor, another door opened onto a generic work floor where three more men sat tinkering with tools and weapons and drinking coffee. In one corner, partially separate thanks to a half-wall, was a desk. The man sat behind it.

"Holmes DeFrieze," he introduced himself. "Operations leader. Who told you we need help? Some pissant little punk fuck who thinks we're getting weaker and his worthless little *vato* friends said it's time to move in on us? Is that it? We've never been in better shape than we are now. We don't *need* anyone's help."

Hyde snorted, and half of his mouth smiled. His eyes did not. "You think I care what punk kids on the street say? I talk to *professionals.*

"*They* say Block 9X is looking for people to push back against some rival operation. It confuses me. They said you guys were hard bastards. How can that be true if you get your goddamn feelings hurt by a few mercs looking to make money?"

DeFrieze's lip curled, but his round face only settled into an unpleasant grin. "I get it. You're here because you're such a hard bastard and you want to see if we measure up to your illustrious standards. Well, I got something for you, friend. Something that ought to answer everyone's questions real fast."

He stood from the desk and pushed a button on a small panel on the wall. "We need an Irondog, five minutes, ten tops."

Someone else replied, "Yes, sir. No problem."

DeFrieze folded his hands behind his broad back. "You know what an Irondog is? You should. You could be one yourself. If you're as good as you think you are."

Nasreen piped up. "Augments?"

The oily man nodded. "Guys we hire for special purposes, who are open-minded. Ex-cons, mainly, sometimes ex-soldiers. Or both. For a nice paycheck and protection from going back to prison where they probably belong, they're willing to sign up for a full physical replacement of meat for metal. Like you, big guy. Our indentured shock troops."

Hyde uttered one of his low, grinding laughs. "I am the last person who would be surprised or intimidated to hear that."

Dante asked, "What are you summoning this man for? To show off his chrome grill?"

Nasreen flashed him a nasty look, and it occurred to Dante that in the last year, he had grown more sarcastic and willing to make jokes, even half-assed ones. His near-death experience with SSS had corroded his all-business demeanor. A little.

DeFrieze stated, "To fight."

Dante had been afraid of that, but he showed no sign of being perturbed.

Hyde kept silent and looked back at the operations leader with his usual amused sneer.

DeFrieze went on, "It's up to you if you still want to be bothered. If you can take down an Irondog hand-to-hand, maybe you're worth enough of a shit to question Block 9X. If you can't, it means you had no right to open your fat mouth, and we'll mount your brain case on the wall. *Comprende?*"

Nasreen let out a slow breath. It might have been an act since pretending to be worried about her friend could potentially make DeFrieze overconfident.

Hyde extended a metal hand. "You got yourself a deal, Mr. DeFrieze."

CHAPTER FOURTEEN

The "sparring room," as Block 9X politely called it, was located in the basement at the compound's center. It was easier to hide anything that went on from detection by the outside world. Most of the company employees, or at least most of those present on-site, had gathered to watch.

Dante scanned them all. Or rather, he let Midas scan them.

The AI's silent inner voice reported, *"So far, none of them match the individuals you encountered at the relay station. Granted, we did not have time to get a very good look at them. I have only fleeting, blurred images and footage, but I believe none of those men are present today."*

He responded with a vague emotional impulse meant to convey *Okay, thanks.* Midas fell silent until further notice.

Dante and Nasreen stood in the rear corner. DeFrieze and his cohorts had conveniently ensured they ended up far from any egress points. When Dante had been about to protest or surreptitiously relocate himself, two guys with dart launchers and razor-fists had suddenly materialized to block him off. He supposed he ought to have known that Block 9X was savvy enough to keep him and Nasreen defanged the whole time, even if they hadn't figured out who the pair was.

Hyde had stripped off his half-assembled weapons and clothes aside from an obligatory pair of trunks. His weirdly ceramic-like body glowed dully under the harsh overhead lights. For the first time, Dante wondered if they hadn't underspent on getting him operational again.

The cyborg implements he and Nasreen had purchased were a step or two above average civilian shit. They weren't top of the line but were pricey by normal standards. The idea had been to get Hyde mobile again so he could use actual weapons and his skills and experience. They had not anticipated him getting involved in melee combat sports.

Dante's heart sank as the Irondog who would be acting as DeFrieze's champion strutted out onto the mat.

When still mostly human, the man had been old enough to have a good amount of know-how behind him. He was still young, probably twenty-eight or so. Hyde was so old that it was amazing he still functioned as well as he did, notwithstanding how much of his body was technically new.

Furthermore, the Irondog's suit appeared to be the latest and greatest in heavy hardware. Thicker armor, hard edges in all the right places to function as natural weapons or defenses, and subtle signs that it was all powered by something that could easily handle the greater load produced by so much mechanical activity. At least Hyde appeared to be a few inches taller.

Mr. Curtidor still lingered near the edge of the mat. Dante sidled up to him without the armed goons doing anything more than watching him.

He spoke in a low voice. "You sure you can do this, Hyde?"

The ex-Reaper made a low, buzzing growl in the back of his throat, like an agitated dog. "Yeah. Having the metal is one thing. Knowing how to use it is another. I'm one of the *first*. I've lived as one of these things since before most of these Ironpups were born. I think more of him is flesh than I am. Heh, heh."

It wasn't as encouraging as Hyde probably meant it to sound, but Dante didn't press him. He stepped back next to Nasreen.

Nasreen only murmured, "It's a good thing our boy thinks so highly of himself."

DeFrieze appeared and spread his hands. "All right, everybody shut up. Now, for the rules. The fight begins when we say and stops when we say, no exceptions. The fight stays on the mat. No fuckin' bystander casualties, okay? That's it." He smirked. "No rules on what you two can do to each other. We'll know when one guy wins because the other guy ain't moving."

Midas opined soundlessly, *"Oh, it is that kind of a fight, is it? I thought they would want to preserve the lives of their people. Or is this one of those 'matters of honor' and they feel sacrificing a life is worth it to avenge an insult?"*

Dante responded, also without speaking aloud, *"I'm not sure. They might cut the fight off before it looks like anyone is about to die. We'll have to wait and see."*

The Irondog had cold eyes and high cheekbones. His suit's electronic and hydraulic elements hummed as he flexed his massive hands. He stepped onto the mat with a short bow.

Hyde did likewise, wearing his usual nasty leer.

DeFrieze made a chopping motion. "Fight."

Something whirred, and there was a flash of motion. Light refracted in all directions as both cyborgs rushed each other at the same time. Their initial movement was too fast for Dante's eye to follow at first. He was well-learned enough as a fighter to guess what was going through their heads. Each man sought to surprise and overwhelm the other, winning the contest as quickly as possible.

Then both stopped as metal *clanked* and shuddered with sudden violence. The Irondog had the upper hand. He was slightly faster despite his heavier suit, and something about the way he carried himself suggested greater baseline strength. His huge arms and thick, jagged knees rained blows on Hyde, who blocked half of them and tanked the rest.

Dante gritted his teeth. A normal man would already have been dead or permanently crippled with a crushed skull, collapsed ribs and lungs, or a broken spine. Hyde was doing no worse than a flesh-and-blood boxer who takes a few decent hits from a padded fist. It still meant his opponent was the one dominating the fight.

The Block 9X men laughed or cheered in low voices. They were too cynical and jaded a bunch to get much enjoyment out of the spectacle, but there wasn't much indication they wanted the interloper to win over their guy. Dante couldn't blame them.

Then a punch from the Irondog abruptly stopped dead with Hyde grasping his arm and locking it into place. The ex-Reaper's fist slammed into the younger man's face while he twisted the arm with his other hand. The Irondog fell back and broke free, shaking his arm and head. He hadn't suffered major damage, but Hyde had sent a clear signal that he would not be an easy opponent after all.

A couple of guys in the audience crooned, "Oooohhh," enjoying the prospect of a real duel rather than a mere beatdown. Hyde and the Irondog clashed again. Their unnaturally fast lunges became a blur, with snapshots in between as Dante tried to "read" the unspoken language of battle.

He deciphered it after a moment's observation. Hyde was allowing the Irondog to throw everything he had at him to take his enemy's measure and get a feel for his capabilities. With a better idea of what he was up against, the ex-Reaper was starting to counterattack, dismantling his opponent's defenses and turning his offenses back against him.

Eduardo H. Curtidor laughed with his usual grinding echoes. "Ha, ha, ha! As I thought. That doesn't work on *me*, boy."

The Irondog had caught Hyde's arm and tried to break it at

the elbow. Hyde let the joint invert and rotated his whole arm around the shoulder cuff. He suddenly stood at his foe's back and punched his sides and neck. The Irondog warded off the blows and elbowed Hyde in the chest. It knocked him back a step or two but didn't do much damage.

Something clicked in Dante's mind. Hyde had replaced almost his *entire* body with machinery. The physical laws of the human body the younger man was still partially beholden to didn't bind him.

For all his youthful vigor and impressive equipment, the Irondog did not know how to maximize the effectiveness of things like unbreakable limb joints. He wasn't locking down moving parts into total immobility. He also hadn't figured out the channels of force application that could overwhelm narrower points of lesser strength and fracture human opponents' hands, feet, and fingers.

As the fight stretched on—for seconds, perhaps minutes, it seemed longer—Hyde systematically exploited every weakness he could find. He disabled parts of the Irondog's limbs, crushed organs or processing centers with carefully located dents, sapped his strength, and cut off his every plan of attack. It was almost horrible to watch. The old cyborg had turned the art of killing with his bare artificial hands into a science.

Finally, desperation grew on the youthful face. The Irondog tried to end the fight with a risky, overextended kick to the face. Hyde caught his ankle, flipped him over, and ripped his entire leg clean off his body in a shower of sparks, oil-blood, and metal fragments. Then he bashed the other man's head with the dismembered limb.

"*Stop!*"

Hyde stopped as DeFrieze stepped in, his face pinkish and flustered, making a horizontal swiping motion.

"Stop," the operations leader repeated. "You win, we get it, good job. Arkoff, take this guy back to the infirmary."

As Hyde stepped back, grinning and breathing heavily, the man called Arkoff dragged the ruined, mostly unconscious form of the Irondog off the mat and out of the sparring room. Someone else picked up his leg and carted it off, too.

Hyde cleared his throat. "So, looks like I—"

DeFrieze interrupted him. "Won for yourself. All three of you want to join, so you need to fight two more guys. One for each of them." He gestured at Dante and Nasreen.

Nasreen had her arms crossed. They fell to her sides as she leaned forward, slack-jawed. "What? That is fucking bullshit. You—"

One of the guys next to her deployed the blade of his razor-fist. He didn't move against her, but they all saw and heard the knife. Trembling with rage, Nasreen shut up and leaned back again, nostrils flaring madly.

Dante didn't blame her. He had half-expected some trickery like this, but it was still galling.

Hyde didn't bat an eye. "Bring them on," he urged. Something in his voice sounded hungry.

DeFrieze motioned as two more Irondogs came into the room. One was thin and sleek, the other at least as bulky as the first one, but otherwise similar. They stepped onto the mat at once.

Nasreen exclaimed, "Hey! You can't make him fight two guys at once. Do you have *any* concept of fair play?" The guy with the deployed razorfist glared at her, but she ignored him.

Dante added, "This is the kind of thing that *damages* your professional reputation, DeFrieze. Someone who wins legitimately looks good. Someone who wins by cheating does not."

Had they not been so badly outnumbered, with so many weapons trained on them, Dante might have held one of Block 9X's men at knifepoint until they agreed to fairer terms. It would have been risky, but it would also have made him feel better.

Instead, he secretly pressed a button on his wrist that buzzed

Ambrose with a signal to bring the shuttle toward their location. If he pressed it again, the pilot would know it was time for an emergency extraction. For now, it was simply a message to be ready.

Smirking, the operations leader quipped, "Hmm, I guess I don't give a shit." Half of his men laughed. "Now, fight." He stepped aside.

This time, Hyde hung back, letting the two Irondogs make the first moves. They had seen the first Irondog when they passed in the hall so they knew they were dealing with a dangerous adversary. Their advance was cautious and strategic. Each moved when the other stopped, trying to exploit the inherent difficulties of fighting multiple people. They stayed far apart, the better to divide Hyde's attention.

Then both pounced at the same instant, one going high, the other low, moving at odd and irregular angles.

Hyde surprised them by plowing straight into the slimmer one. He took a nasty blow to the knee but slammed his fists into the smaller man's skull and tossed him aside.

The bigger one moved in and practically knocked Hyde over with a heavy kick, but the ex-Reaper spun from the follow-up blow with surprising nimbleness and cracked him on the jaw. Then all three cyborgs went into overdrive. Their motions came so fast that Dante had to hope Midas could analyze it better than he.

Sensing the thought, the AI reported, *"Hyde is sending minor coded signals to indicate that he has the situation under control. Perhaps he is incorrect, but at least he believes he can still win."*

Dante maintained an emotionless straight face. *"Okay, then. Let's see him deliver on that promise."*

He watched as Hyde changed up his tactics. He shifted from defense to offense, unexpectedly doing things that seemed stupid but caught his foes by surprise, fighting like a cornered animal, wearing them down with sheer savage ferocity as much as skill or finesse.

Half of the onlookers gasped as Hyde launched an uppercut at the big guy, sending him reeling, and stomped on the smaller guy's back hard enough to break something within and leave him twitching in spasms on the floor.

Then he jumped at the other man, clinging to his shoulders and pulling him off-balance. He came perilously close to losing by ring-out but righted his course at the last instant. The Irondog groaned and snarled, desperate now until at last Hyde sharply twisted his head and his body began to stiffen.

Dante muttered, "Good lord."

Hyde let his opponent slump to the floor. He didn't seem to be dead, although the neck-snapping would have killed a mere human. It would probably put the Irondog out of commission for weeks. The slender one, too, was damaged to the point of being crippled until Block 9X could repair him. The fight was over.

DeFrieze gawked. He was out of dirty tricks to pull, short of simply ordering his men to swarm Hyde and murder him.

The ex-Reaper strode off the mat toward the wall mounting where the chromed trophy skulls lay—Dante recalled the operations leader's little threat when he first made the offer.

Hyde reached out, snatched a skull, and hurled it at DeFrieze. It sped through the air too fast for the man to block or dodge. He took it in the upper chest and shoulder area and fell over backward, landing on the floor with a heavy *thud*.

The crowd roiled, and the air thickened with their growls and oaths. Dante had seen brawls and massacres happen, and his stomach felt like it was sinking out the bottom of his body and falling into a pit. "Oh, fuck," he lamented. Nasreen, too, was tense and prepared for the worst.

The door burst open as knives and batons cleared belts all around the chamber. In strode a compact, muscular older man in a paramilitary uniform, flanked by two security guards. "Hey —*Hey!*" he roared. "Knock this shit off. *Stand down!*"

Everyone froze in place, and the cloud of hostility lifted. Weapons returned to holsters, and the men eased their stances. Dante exhaled gently, not wanting his relief to look too obvious.

The newcomer marched over to DeFrieze and grabbed his arm. "Pick yourself up, DeFrieze." He gave a sharp tug, and the oily man rose to his feet.

He was not as badly damaged as Dante expected, due perhaps to luck, or maybe the skull hadn't had the mass or velocity to do much harm. He still looked furious and uncomfortable.

DeFrieze sputtered, "Sorry, Company Commander."

The officer glared around at everyone else. "I know what's going on. You don't have to explain it all to me. It damn well looks like they passed the test. Fold these three into the next briefing. We've suddenly got three Irondogs incapacitated, so it will help to have replacements, won't it?"

He spun on his heel and stormed out.

The rest of Block 9X kept quiet as a ruffled DeFrieze advanced toward Dante while still shuddering with suppressed rage. He pretended to ignore Hyde, who stood off to the side, sneering at him.

"Okay," DeFrieze droned. "I'm giving you the codes to tap into our message line. Give them to anyone else, and you're dead. Yes, the company commander would approve of that. Check the line tomorrow for a call. You'll probably be in on an operation soon."

Dante punched in the codes as DeFrieze showed him. Then he offered a polite smile and nodded. "Much appreciated."

CHAPTER FIFTEEN

They waited.

Hyde called from the corner, "Are we there yet?" He chuckled at his wit, then returned to what he'd been doing—tinkering with a homebrew customization to his fearsome metal body. He'd been busy with repairs after the fight and was taking the opportunity to fine-tune several things. Plus adding more artistic and cosmetic touches to make himself look still more intimidating.

Dante looked over all the equipment on the table for the eleventh or twelfth time that afternoon. He replied in a monotone, "No, Hyde. We are not anywhere yet, except here."

"It was a joke." The cyborg talked to himself in low, burbling Spanish and turned back to his affairs.

The four of them had sequestered themselves in a rented suite of rooms in a midrange hotel. It was the kind of place that could offer them decent living accommodations and privacy but without attracting too much scrutiny or breaking the bank. They could also access the rooms from outdoors, which made it easier to bring equipment in and out without having cameras and guards all over them.

However, Nuevo Rio was the type of city where they could

have bribed the guards if that's what it ended up taking. Fortunately, they hadn't needed to.

Since morning, each of them had drifted into a different roster of tasks to prepare for the upcoming rigors. It also helped them cope with the unappealing mixture of stress and boredom that always accompanied situations like this.

Predictably, Midas was shopping. He would intrude upon Dante's thoughts with questions about whether or not he could buy something or suggestions for new items that might help them. To his credit, at least he was recommending things that would benefit them all, rather than only upgrades for himself.

Still, Dante said "no" nine times out of ten. Their funds were substantial but not unlimited. Accounting for an endless flow of new stuff only distracted them from maximizing what they already had.

Hyde was working on himself, in between complaining or trying to make jokes in the hope that someone would get mad at him. In the absence of violence, he considered petty arguments a decent substitute. They all knew him too well to bother taking the bait.

Nasreen had settled in before her sphere at a small desk in the corner opposite Hyde. She searched constantly and obsessively for new information and data regarding the kidnappers who'd stolen the apprentices out from under her.

As upset as she was, Dante suspected the emotions she'd shown openly were only the tip of the iceberg. She must have been truly devastated by the experience. It was the one thing she returned to in the absence of *anything* else that required her attention.

Dante was prepping all the equipment he could think of, double-checking it, ensuring everything was in good working order, and trying to account for every possible contingency in advance. There was no way to be prepared for *everything*, but if he could at least be ready for ninety percent of it, he could usually improvise on the last ten.

Ambrose was in the other room, vegetating in front of a viewscreen showing some asinine cooking stream.

Since Dante had exhausted his equipment's possibilities, he leaned back and started mentally reviewing all the facts concerning Block 9X. He'd learned a great deal during their misadventure yesterday.

The company commander who'd saved them from an all-out melee was named Miguel Sheer. He seemed halfway sensible and had real authority in the organization, so he was someone to keep in mind.

Before Dante could reflect on anything else, Nasreen exhaled a characteristic raspy sigh and got up. She walked to his table and sat next to him.

"Dante. I don't understand it. It's like they're ghosts." She collapsed her sphere into a compact rectangle but did not slide it into her pocket. "I give up on finding anything more. The kidnappers might as well not exist. Braelin, Neburu, and Mugoi have vanished from reality."

The Marauder looked down at his rangy hands. A pang of something hit him in the gut, taking him five or ten seconds to recognize it as guilt. Guilt and concern.

"I believe you about what happened. They exist, and so do our apprentices. We'll find them. Network surfing isn't going to turn up everything we need. People like that who could pull off an operation like the one that netted them are going to have ways of covering their tracks."

She probably knew that, but he'd figured out by now that she liked it when he said things out loud when she was feeling discouraged.

She sat up a little straighter. "Yes, true. It's one more frustration on top of others. I specialize in this sort of thing." She turned the collapsed sphere over in her hands, unable to decide whether to begin trawling for clues again.

Dante speculated, "If this job that Block 9X has for us is against them, we're heading in the right direction. We'll find them."

Hyde agreed, "Yeah, we will. I don't know or care about them, but if you want them found, I can do it."

Nasreen stood. "If that's true, you're a much better person than you used to be, Eduardo."

He snorted. "Don't call me that. But thanks, I guess. How does this look?" He flexed the back of his hand, where he had been etching a jagged, symmetrical design that might have been an attempt at a tribal tattoo.

"Good," Nasreen stated flatly. "Remember that tattoos are expensive to remove, so be careful with them."

He laughed. "Yes, Mother."

Nasreen looked back and forth between the cyborg in the corner and the man at the table. "Both of you have changed so much. You don't seem to realize it, but it's true." Her gentle tone and bright eyes suggested she did not mean it as a criticism.

Dante looked up at her. "Oh? What do you mean by that?"

She put her hands on her hips. "I used to think—perceive, intuit, whatever term you want to use—that each of you was a selfish or self-centered person. To a greater or lesser extent." She looked at Hyde, then back at Dante.

"So?" Hyde scoffed. "It's not as though I pretended to be otherwise."

Dante said nothing. He hadn't thought of it that way. It would have taken him time to think it over and come up with an intelligent response, so he kept his mouth shut for the moment.

Nasreen went on. "Yet now, you are devoting and investing all your time, energy, and personal resources into *this*. You're risking your lives for people who once we've saved them will not be able to reward you with staggering amounts of money, which was your usual motivation for doing dangerous things. They'll probably require more of you once we find them."

Hyde seemed annoyed by the spiel and glowered at his tools.

Dante broke his silence. "I suppose that's true. I don't really understand the point you're trying to make. You know I'm not, um, good with emotions and stuff."

Nasreen brushed his shoulder. "You're getting a little better all the time. For me... I wonder if it's like a misplaced biological thing. It's almost like being a parent. We took them under our care to mentor them." There was an unusual note in her voice, tenderness mixed with pain.

Dante shook his head. "Maybe, but I doubt it. I don't feel anything that seems like a 'biological imperative.' It's only the duty of being responsible for them as a teacher. They trusted us, we pledged to help each other, and they're probably in the current situation because they were with us. Going after them is the right thing to do. I can't say it makes me feel like I'm their father."

A short, breathy sound indicated she hadn't wanted to hear that. "You always take everything literally."

Hyde explained in a more subdued tone than usual, "I'm in it for you two. You did stuff for me, gave me a new life. You didn't have to. I'm here to help out until you decide we're done." His voice sank to a groan of embarrassment. "Although I *guess* you could say that I like helping people with shit. Since I've been living Dirtside. It's all different down there."

Dante chuckled. "It's more your sort of place. Less civilized."

"Yeah. Fuck. Playing the bad guy is still fun, sometimes. Sounded fun when you pitched the idea the other day. But to be honest, I don't want to keep being that monster. You two showed me I could be more than that. So, I owe you. I'm honoring your gift."

Nasreen stared at him, blinking. "You've changed *much* more than I thought, Hyde."

Ambrose called from the adjacent room, "You people are all much nobler than I am. I want to get this over with and go back to flying Dirtside. I like doing things I'm familiar with, and that is all."

"Hah!" Hyde guffawed. "Bullshit, Am. There's some Dirtwalker *chica* you like, isn't there? You can't hide it from me forever. I *will* know, and you will *never* hear the end of it."

Dante snickered. He had to admit the thought was strangely funny. Dirtwalker women didn't seem much like Ambrose's type.

Am protested, "Hey, now. That's none of your business. I only work these days. I don't have time for that sort of thing." He sounded genuinely flustered. Dante couldn't be sure if that was because what Hyde said was true or because the presumption aggravated him. Nasreen would probably know. She was better at reading people than he was.

Before he could ask her, a single chiming sound rose and echoed through the room.

Midas spoke aloud. "That is our signal, everyone. Block 9X has issued the mission and coordinates. It's good to see that they're being thorough."

CHAPTER SIXTEEN

Nasreen had no desire to go back to Block 9X's headquarters in Nuevo Rio after the incident the other day. Hyde had pulled through, but it was still a desperately ugly and frightening situation.

Not only the danger but the way DeFrieze had deliberately tried to demoralize them, cheating to their faces and daring them to do anything about it. She looked forward to never seeing him again if it was possible.

It was a relief when the mercenaries wanted them to rendezvous at the job site for the briefing and other concerns.

The downside was that the message was terse and extremely vague about what they would be doing or why. It made sense. They didn't want any scanners or hackers to pick up keywords to retain plausible deniability for as long as possible. Still, she would have liked to know more in advance.

Dante didn't seem overly concerned. "The location sounds right," he'd observed as they had boarded the shuttle bus that would take them back to Atlantica Central. "Based on my previous run-in with these guys."

He was referring to his relay substation event while Nasreen struggled to protect her charges from the kidnappers.

Their rendezvous point was a grav-line hub station for a few different routes. It was most notable for running right to a compartment located *below* Atlantica where there were power plants and processing centers. Those connected the solar panels on the city's underside with various networks throughout the Station.

As Dante had put it, "Can't have communications without power." This led Hyde to make a halfhearted scary comment about how the real power lay in force, but it seemed to be him playing a character again.

Ambrose had hung back again. His role was to pilot their shuttle and remain out of sight but ready to intervene at the appropriate time. Only Nasreen, Dante, and Mr. Curtidor rode the bus to the grav-line.

When they arrived and disembarked, the small crowd was mostly employees about to start their evening shift. Few passengers got off at this point, and the little station seemed designed with only the lightest and most cursory traffic in mind. It lacked much in the way of space or luxuries.

The trio found the specified lounge area in one of the station's wings easily enough. Their contacts were waiting for them.

Nasreen's heart sank. She had allowed herself to hope against hope that the team's commander would be anyone other than Holmes DeFrieze.

"Well, nice to see you guys again," DeFrieze gloated as they strolled in. "I bet you're looking forward to all the fun we're gonna have, right? Oh, and don't worry, we rented the room out so there'll be no unexpected visitors, and our guy already scanned it for bugs. You may speak freely. Heh, heh."

A dozen of Block 9X's finest were with him, including two more Irondogs. The rest were normal men but fearsome looking with grim expressions and cold eyes. They wore the types of suits sometimes used by average security firms or certain types of external maintenance crews who had to spacewalk or do other dangerous tasks.

It meant they were well-equipped and well-outfitted, but most people wouldn't immediately recognize them as a mercenary strike force about to engage in a highly illegal gang war operation.

Hyde was back to pretending to be their leader and point man. "Good, I hate having to be all coy. Where are we going and who do we kill? That's the essence of it, isn't it?"

Dante chimed in. "Usually is, yeah."

Ignoring the Marauder, DeFrieze elaborated, "Kinda, my friend. The devil is in the details. Listen the fuck up so I don't have to repeat myself and you don't get any of these fine men killed, right?"

Hyde grinned at the entire team. "That's right. We hope everyone has fun."

DeFrieze explained that their rivals were known for sending out elite abduction teams. Fixating on that detail, Nasreen took heart. They were on the right track to finding the apprentices.

Block 9X had managed to capture one of the kidnappers and interrogate him, using advanced and reliable methods.

Nasreen quipped, "I'm impressed that you guys don't torture people. That shit doesn't work half the time."

Irritated at the aside, DeFrieze snapped, "We fuckin' know, okay? Now let me talk. So, once we're confident that this guy is telling the truth, he spills out the whole thing. Not only methods but infrastructure and context stuff..."

The substation they'd be going to had a series of compartments attached that were not part of the original construction. They were easily visible from space or certain obscure viewpoints in Atlantica's underbelly. The entrances to the compartments were almost impossible to find from within the main structure unless one knew where to look.

DeFrieze concluded, "They're using this place as a base, or it's one of their cash cows, like a fraud factory or hacking hub, who knows. It's important to them, and they guard the hell out of it. Our purpose is to get in there, kill everybody, and disrupt things as much as possible. Send them a clear message not to mess with us while they spend a year or two recouping their losses. It's a nice simple job."

A few of the mercs laughed in a subtly nasty way. Dante pretended to smile, and Nasreen contented herself with a nod.

DeFrieze clapped his meaty hands. "Everyone do your last-minute prep. We move out in four minutes."

Dante had to ask, "What's the battle plan? Formations, tactics, rules of engagement, floor plans for the place we're going into? We need to know all that stuff."

DeFrieze glared at him hatefully. "We assume you already know how to fight through a building. If you don't, you're not worth anything to us. We'll get you your precious floor plan.

"Formation is whatever I say it is after I see what's up when we get there. ROE is that anything moving gets put down unless it's some idiot's four-year-old daughter or some crap. Otherwise, it's a 'let God sort 'em out' type of mission."

Hyde's smile was downright disturbing. "I missed this. Thank you, Mr. DeFrieze, for giving me this wonderful opportunity."

When the Block 9X guys chortled again, it sounded like even they were a tad unsettled.

Dante turned his head toward Nasreen and whispered, "This is going to be a shitshow. Remember everything I taught you. I'll remember everything you taught me."

She inhaled. "Yes, that's about the best we can do."

They spent a few moments preparing their weapons, mostly hidden under their coats in various pieces, for rapid deployment once they got on-site and checking to ensure that everyone's headset had linked into the same comms frequency. Then DeFrieze distributed fake security badges, which they all pinned on their lapels, and the whole group moved out.

Nasreen gave a tug on the sleeves of Dante and Hyde, holding them back for a second. Something had occurred to her, and they might not get another opportunity to discuss it.

"Hey. It makes sense now. Between what they said and what you said, Dante, about the place you were at before."

Hyde rasped, "What the fuck?"

Dante kept quiet and listened.

Nasreen continued. "The abduction teams. They've been able to hide their presence so effectively because they're based at a place that acts as a hub of massive energy dispersal. So much power passes through that it masks their communications and any signals their devices might give off.

"Not to mention, they can coordinate their actions and send messages by tapping into all devices in Atlantica Central. They'd have access to everything. They can cover their tracks by scrambling all records of their actions or any tracing signals right at the source."

DeFrieze shouted, "Hey! Move it. This train is leaving."

The three started toward the platform, moving at a fast clip but not quite hurrying. None of them wanted to give their temporary commander the satisfaction of thinking he could intimidate them.

Dante commented, "I'd say you're right about that. You have more experience than I do when it comes to espionage stuff. Puts things in perspective. Once we get there, it will take *all* our experience to deal with whatever they have in store for us."

A grav-train had arrived, one of the few that went to the substation controlled by the kidnapping cartel. DeFrieze boarded half of his men first, then Hyde, Dante, and Nasreen, and himself along with the other half of the 9X team. There were no other passengers in the compartment. Like most public transportation these days, the train was automated. They were alone.

There was some low chatter among the troops for the first few minutes. Then DeFrieze raised his voice, telling everyone to be quiet, and he squeezed around to the front of the compartment where he could address everyone at once.

"All right," he barked. "It's a tradition that the newbies take point." He smiled and pointed at Hyde, waving his finger to indicate Nasreen and Dante. "When we get there, we expect you to breach the place—after all you're so tough and resilient—and also to properly warn us about any issues the rest of the team might encounter."

Nasreen suspected the type of "warning" the operations leader had in mind was seeing their smoking corpses slump midway into the battle. What he didn't realize was that he was helping their main goal.

DeFrieze thought he was hanging them out to dry, punishing them for their insolence. Having the trio out in front meant they would be the first to decide how to deal with whatever they found—and for their purposes, this was a search-and-rescue mission, not a destructive reprisal.

If the apprentices were at the substation, Hyde, Dante, or Nasreen would be first to encounter them. If they were not—although she hoped desperately that wasn't the case—at least they would be able to collect or destroy any evidence or information before Block 9X could get their paws on it.

Dante ignored the sadistic leers of the men around them. "That sounds fair. It means we're not dependent on anyone else's competence in assessing the situation."

Hyde laughed. "Exactly."

Nasreen could not be certain, but it looked like the rows of smirks dimmed at that.

They had another advantage, unspoken but well-known to all three. Ambrose would be there in the shuttle, running dark, ready to swoop in and pick them up for a quick getaway as soon as Dante or Nasreen sent him the appropriate message.

Ambrose was neither courageous nor exceedingly loyal, and Nasreen sometimes wondered why Dante had put up with the man for as long as he had. His recent promise to come through for them, to do what he was supposed to, seemed sincere enough. If nothing else, he feared what Dante would do if betrayed a *third* time.

They would have to trust him and wait.

Hyde asked, "Are we going to try an infiltration, or do we go guns blazing right away? I don't care either way. I'm sure the guns will blaze no matter what. It's a question of how long it takes."

DeFrieze's mouth twisted in disgust and exasperation, as though Hyde had no right to ask such a reasonable question and was stupid for even thinking of it.

"The half-assed uniforms and fake badges are to get us close enough to where they don't have time to hit the alarm before we start taking them out. Once we *are* close enough, there's not much point in all the dissembling and shit. They won't buy it anyway. Kill the bastards at the first sign of trouble so we can storm in nice and quick-like."

Hyde grinned horribly once again. "Good."

CHAPTER SEVENTEEN

Few grav-trains or buses went to the underside of the Stations, whether Atlantica Central or any other. In general, the bottoms of the domes were for complex and obscure machinery. Specialized crews who did occasional routine inspections or went out to deal with specific problems handled them and kept them up.

They were not for average citizens, sightseers, tourists, or high society. The only other persons besides tech and maintenance employees who could reasonably be expected were security officers.

Dante thought there was something inherently disturbing about an environment where the void of space was below one's feet and a huge mass of solid material was above one's head.

The computerized voice system within the train announced, "Substation 17-A, estimated arrival time two minutes." It repeated the message in a half-dozen other languages.

DeFrieze looked around. "Everybody got that? Again, we all know our positions. We break through to the main rear control room. That's where all the extra compartments branch off from." He nodded at Hyde. "Once our point men get us in there, either me or Svenko will open the secret door, and that's when the real fun begins. Get ready, and don't fuck up."

Dante was fairly certain that Svenko was one of the other Irondogs. It would make sense to have one of the more resilient members of the team be responsible for one of the most important aspects of the mission.

The grav-train glided to a stop. They had emerged from the main body of the entire city-station and were in a covered and reinforced tube looping around the lower curve of it. The substation extended off into space like a stunted limb.

Much of the material around them was clear as crystal, the same stuff used in the sky-domes, except it lacked the artificial lighting features. It was mostly blackness around them with the stars, the Earth below, and the distant sprawl of the other Stations.

The avenue leading to the substation was a metal walkway covered with a tall, broad cylinder of transparent material. Dante noted that the extra compartments were difficult to see from here. When the kidnappers' group or whoever was behind them had added to the structure, they'd done so in a way to keep the additions hidden whenever someone got close enough to examine things in detail.

This suggested that the mysterious organization controlling the place was fairly savvy. Nasreen's earlier comments about their clever means of disguising their movements and communications sprang to mind.

At least everyone was wearing helmets. Any security cameras within the facility would have great difficulty picking up faces. They'd have only the fake security nametags to go on. The people in charge of the organization were probably smart enough to recognize that the tags were illegitimate. There was still a good chance they would waste precious time checking into each name they saw when reviewing the footage later.

DeFrieze quipped, "Remember to have fun, boys and girls. Especially you three."

The doors opened, and Hyde was the first out with Dante and Nasreen following at his elbows. The rest of the 9X force waited a moment and filed out in what might have looked like laziness or disorganization to an observer. It wasn't. They were carefully timing their movements.

At the end of the walkway were the substation's double doors. Dante could not see any special security measures on them. Surprises might lay in wait, but they seemed to be standard stuff. Difficult to breach without the right equipment if put in emergency seal mode, but otherwise not a serious problem.

Two guards out front had emerged from the building as the grav-train pulled up and they realized they had visitors. Both wore unremarkable, mid-grade body armor and half-helmets along with dark glasses. They had batons on their belts, and one appeared to have a dart launcher on his wrist.

Hyde roared, "Hey, guys! We're the new security detail. Did they already clear us, or will we have to go through all that stupid fucking scan everything, punch in all the numbers shit? Ha, ha."

The pair of men stood in place, looking back and forth between each other and the approaching group. One of them hit a button and opened the doors, stepping back through them, possibly to hit an alarm or at least to page his supervisors about what to do about unexpected guests.

The ruse wasn't working too well, Dante decided. He threw off his coat, let half of his smart rifle fall into his hands, and pulled the other half off his back, snapping them together in the same motion. It wasn't easy given the weapon's weight, but he managed it.

The guard who'd remained on the walkway stumbled backward as his face contorted with horror. "No, no, no!" He raised his arm and fired a dart at Hyde.

Hyde had mimicked Dante by shrugging off his coat and

quick-assembling his gun. The dart crumpled against his metal chest. Then he and Dante both raised their weapons.

The smart rifles crackled with massive, thunderous intensity, lighting up the dim transparent corridor with their star-shaped muzzle flares. They were loaded with the "soft," frangible ammunition. Using the hard stuff while Station-bound would have been the height of madness.

The guard out front danced and twisted under the barrage, the rounds ripping through the unarmored parts of his body and denting his armor inward where it did strike. He fell, spewing blood from half a dozen points.

Hyde rushed forward and caught the doors before they could close. The second guard within had caught most of the bullets that had bypassed his comrade. He lay dying in a heap on the floor. Hyde stomped on his head, crunching his helmet and finishing him off.

Dante rushed forward. "Hyde, hold the door."

The cyborg growled without words, annoyed at being given such a mundane task as Dante sprinted down the short corridor beyond and checked all the electronics. There was no obvious sign of trouble. He kicked open the second door and glanced down the diagonal halls branching from it.

Men advanced from both directions, two to the left and one to the right. They had shock batons and razorfists and seemed surprised by the sight of an actual firearm.

Midas announced, *"I've got this!"* They had synchronized the smart rifle's AI with Dante's implanted second intelligence, which meant that Midas could help operate the gun's targeting system.

Green circles appeared on all three men, conjured by Midas's visual interface, and crosshairs formed within the circles. Dante raised the rifle and fired, aiming for the two to the left first.

He squeezed off a burst, not aiming too hard, and was impressed when the smart bullets left curving streaks in the air as they veered around toward the guards' centers of mass. The rounds battered and punctured their chest cavities or tore open their throats, and both collapsed.

Dante had barely swung the rifle to the right when he fired again, this time blinking to readjust the target and place it on the third man's head. The bullets arced upward, two of them catching the poor bastard in the face. The result was a red cloud, with his helmet toppling off and the rest of him flying back to land flat on the floor.

Nasreen rushed up and over the threshold. She had taken out her weapon, a high-end stun gun with the power turned to maximum. It was intended for serious crowd control and would create electrical pulses that could severely disable or kill up to seven or eight people within a distance of thirty-five feet or less. Its effectiveness waned beyond that point. They didn't expect to be fighting much at longer distances.

"Out of the way, Hyde," she snapped, stepping over one of his legs.

Hyde retorted with a stream of rasping Spanish, which she ignored. Rushing to the control panel past the main doors, she punched a couple of buttons and took a moment to scan something with her sphere. "Okay. Alarm system down. They heard all the gunfire, I'm sure. We don't know how many people they have here, but the bulk of their forces are probably within the secret part of the facility."

By now, DeFrieze and his men had caught up. "Nicely done," the leader called, and he almost sounded sincere about it. "Now quit wasting time. Onward, you fucks."

Dante asked, "Which way to the main control room?" He didn't care if Nasreen, DeFrieze, Svenko, or someone else was the one to answer.

Nasreen responded, "Both ways go there, but right would take us closer to the rest of the facility so reinforcements would come from that direction quicker."

Before Dante could suggest the same, DeFrieze bellowed, "HDH or whatever you call yourself, take the right with half of my men behind you. Everyone else, take the left and reconvene in the control room."

Svenko the Irondog took over door-holding duties as Hyde plunged down the rightward corridor and five 9X men followed him. Dante and Nasreen led the charge down the other hall.

There wasn't time to do a systematic room-clearing operation, so Dante had to hope the 9Xers were competent enough to deal with anyone who might try to ambush and flank them from a side chamber. They stomped past doors, ignoring everything except the way forward to their destination.

Halfway there, two guards—a man and a woman—burst out of a door. The man had a dart launcher. The woman had a shotgun, probably loaded with rubber or beanbag shells.

Nasreen was the first to fire. A faint blue-white glow erupted from her stun gun with a loud buzzing and crackling. Both guards dropped their weapons as sparks and steam rose along their armor, and their muscles seized up.

The pair waited a second for the electrical charge to disperse, then shoved the disoriented guards aside—knowing full well that DeFrieze's men would probably cut their throats when they got to them.

A body flew through the air at a juncture ahead. Hyde must have grabbed hold of someone and tossed them. The airborne person slammed into a door and knocked it open. Beyond lay a broad hexagonal chamber, the control room, filled with blinking machines.

Dante ran ahead, taking the lead over Nasreen or Hyde. When he crossed the threshold, two terrified technicians leapt to their feet and pulled out small pistol crossbows. They never got the chance to pull the triggers. Dante shot them both. A single burst from the smart rifle automatically divvied up its rounds between them. Both technicians spun, fell, and exhaled their death rattles.

As the 9X men filed in behind them, another door opened and a couple more guards piled out. Their faces were livid with desperation as they swung their batons. Dante realized the place's security forces were badly unprepared for an assault of this magnitude. He almost felt sorry for them.

One of DeFrieze's men swung a carbon-blade baton and sliced through the first guard's midsection, so his upper half toppled free of his waist in a shower of blood. Svenko grabbed the second's head and crushed it with his hands, helmet and all.

With the control room secured, DeFrieze barged ahead and went to the far wall. Machinery whirred a second later, and a large panel slid aside to reveal a tighter and darker hallway beyond.

"Point men!" DeFrieze barked. "Do your thing. Oh, and it's going to get harder from here. Good luck." Once again, he looked pleased with himself at the prospect of sending them to their deaths.

Midas offered a handy silent reminder. *I have the door's frequency, sir. Once we're through, I'll slam it directly.*

"Good," Dante said aloud. It functioned as a reply to both DeFrieze and Midas.

The magazine in his rifle was currently nearly empty. He ejected it, saved it, and replaced it with a fresh one. The guns had not come with as much smart ammo as he would have preferred, but it might still be enough to see them through.

He and Nasreen went through shoulder-to-shoulder with Hyde guarding their rear more against their "partners" than anything else. Block 9X watched them advance, waiting.

Hyde turned, grinned at DeFrieze, and loudly exclaimed, "Oops!"

Midas shut the door, activating the emergency locking protocol at the same time. DeFrieze's smug expression evaporated as the portal slammed shut in his face, sealing itself before any Block 9X troops could reach it.

Nasreen remarked, "It will be nice to have some privacy while we look for our friends. Although we are also now without backup."

"I know," Dante grumbled. "Move on."

It was apparent that the floor plan from this point on consisted of a concentric oval pattern of short halls. They connected to at least two or three larger compartments, which could have been shuttle bays, storage areas, or laboratories. It was hard to be sure. The trio stomped through the first few corridors before encountering resistance at the door to the first major chamber.

Someone fired a stun pulse at them, similar to what Nasreen's weapon created.

"Shit!" Dante exclaimed, throwing himself aside.

Hyde was not so lucky. The electrical field engulfed him, rattling his teeth and paralyzing him.

Nasreen came up around his side and fired her stun gun through the open door. The effects of the first pulse masked the firing of the second, and men beyond the door screamed.

Dante concentrated on the sounds of their voices and fired a burst of frangible rounds through the opening, blind. The bullets curved in mid-flight and cut through the air around the corner, ending most of the cries of pain.

Hyde freed himself as the electrical field dissipated. "*Pendejos!* That hurt." He plunged through the door snarling, and Dante and Nasreen heard the unpleasant sounds of grinding metal and crunching bones.

Following him, they saw a group of people, possible civilians, vanishing around a corner up ahead. Dante nearly shot them but decided against it. He could not positively identify them as threats, and his team still didn't know where their apprentices were.

He spoke into his headset. "Ambrose, it looks like these guys have an evacuation protocol. You see anything?"

The pilot replied, "Yes! At least two shuttles preparing to launch from opened bays on the outer compartments. It looks like you are right next to the first one."

Without further words, Dante sprinted into the next chamber.

The hall opened onto a short walkway with a railing and staircase leading down to a medium-sized dock. A shuttle in the early stages of powering up waited there. A cluster of guards was escorting a small group toward the craft. A small group of three.

Nasreen gasped. "It's them. They're alive."

Dante pointed at the apprentices as the whole mass of people below noticed their intrusion. "Hyde, those three are our people. Don't hurt them, okay?" Braelin, Jolo, and Mugoi were easy to distinguish from the others. They wore no helmets and were all distinctive-looking persons.

Hyde snorted, reached out and grabbed the railing, and swung himself over it, vaulting up and then allowing the weight of his metal body to pull him down, knowing he could take the fall easier than a nonaugmented human could.

Dante and Nasreen lacked any such capability, but their armor at least offered them some minor impact protection. They took the stairs with Dante charging down, rifle shouldered, and Nasreen behind him with her stun gun.

Dante barked, "Nobody move, or you're dead!" The helmet distorted his voice. The instant the words left his mouth, Hyde *clanked* as he got up from the floor and approached the group from another angle, pinning them down between two intersecting lines of fire.

Braelin, Neburu, and Mugoi, clustered rear and center with the security detail around them in a semicircle, looked as dismayed and confused as any of the station's personnel. They likely had no idea what was happening or why.

Before Dante could identify himself one of the guards decided to throw his life away.

"No!" Dante shouted, but it was too late. The man lunged for him, his baton crackling at full power. Had Dante been only a little slower, he might have successfully disabled him. Instead, Dante turned the rifle on the man and pumped two rounds into his chest. Red wounds caved in by the frangible rounds opened as he fell back, dropping his baton to spark against the floor.

Then everyone else attacked in unison. Everyone.

Nasreen uttered a wordless cry as Jolo Neburu pounced at her and kicked her in the stomach. It knocked her back before she could stun any of the other combatants. Braelin raised his fists, ready to do what he could unarmed. Mugoi leapt atop the shuttle and scuttled over it to intercept Hyde, who roared and charged in.

Again Dante yelled, "No, no, dammit! We're here to rescue you!"

The security people plunged into the fray. Batons and carbon knives flashed through the air. Dante used the butt of his rifle to knock one man's blade-hand aside before elbowing him in the face and shot another in the leg, dropping him screaming to one knee.

Then he was face-to-face with Braelin. The small man was wily and ferocious despite his size and advancing age. He waded in with a shocking lack of fear as his fists lashed toward Dante's visor, throat, groin, and armpits.

Dante turned and pivoted, taking the punches on the harder parts of his armor, and Klement's knuckles were bleeding when he retracted his hands.

"Braelin, it's me, dammit! Dante. And Nasreen. We're saving you, you morons!"

Braelin paused. Another of the kidnappers moved in, trying to launch a dart into Dante's neck at nearly point-blank range. Dante swiveled and drove the rifle's heavy barrel into the guard's midsection before he tripped him and tossed him aside.

Then Dante grabbed his helmet and ripped it off. It exposed

him to the danger of major injury, but he had little choice. The apprentices all seemed to think the newcomers were more their enemies than their captors were.

Klement's eyes bulged. "Holy ever-loving crap, it is you. Neburu! Mugoi! Hold it. You guys, too, wait!"

Nasreen had been fighting Jolo and another guard, keeping on the defensive, trying to separate the two so she could shock the latter without injuring the apprentice. Neburu froze and grabbed her erstwhile comrade's arm to stop him from swinging his baton into Nasreen's face. "Stop!" she insisted.

Nasreen tore her helmet off as well. "See? Good lord, you weren't easy to find. What the hell are you doing?"

Mugoi had managed to drop-kick Hyde, driving the giant back a couple of steps but not hurting him. The battle between the apprentice's incredible speed and agility and Hyde's superior size and strength abruptly halted. Neither of them had any reason to trust one another—they'd never met—but Mugoi saw his mentors and stood down. He looked a touch disappointed.

Hyde leered at him. "Damn. You'd probably have put up a good fight, too."

"Yes, I would have."

Dante stepped forward as the security goons, afraid and hostile but holding back for now fell back a few steps.

"Why are you guys protecting them?" he demanded. "Or did you assume we were here to kill you all? Either way, we need to get out. I've got Ambrose, our pilot, coming in directly."

Braelin and Jolo exchanged a glance. The former said, "Not that easy, boss man. You got the wrong idea about these people."

Nasreen's jaw fell open. "What? They fucking kidnapped you! Remember?"

"Yes, but they had an excellent reason," Neburu chimed in.

CHAPTER EIGHTEEN

Dante groaned. "We don't have much time. The guys we came here with are *not* nice people, and they *are* planning to kill everyone. They got caught up behind a door we closed in their faces, but they'll probably blast through in a minute. Still, why the hell are you so resistant to being rescued? Helsinki Syndrome?"

"Stockholm," Mugoi called from the other side of the shuttle. "No, that is not it."

Braelin explained, "These guys, yeah, they used brutal methods to bring us in, but they didn't have much choice. They're part of a group that calls itself Firewall. They're working in secret against the Voices, Dante. Don't pretend like you don't know what I mean. We overheard you and Nasreen arguing over the Voices a couple of times. Except we know what the hell it means now."

It was Dante's turn to be shocked. With all the commotion, he'd nearly forgotten about the disembodied force that had possessed Midas a year ago—the cause, in some ways, of their whole current dilemma.

Jolo added, "What you call the Voices, they call the Omega

Syndrome. Firewall knew from their intelligence gathering that this entity had contacted you and Nasreen. They have been watching you for months, but they were surprised not to see the corruptive behavior, the abuses of power that are typical and expected of people who have contact with Omega."

Hyde rumbled, "What the goddamn hell is she talking about?"

Dante looked toward him. "The spiders, Hyde. Remember that? You told us about big spiders weaving a web through Atlantica. I've been trying to figure out what you meant by that ever since. It sounds like these people might have the answer."

One of the wounded security guards glared up at the Marauder. "You killed half of our people here!" Tears of pain were forming in his eyes.

Dante frowned. "I'm sorry. Why the fuck didn't you people contact us the normal way, then? When you spy on someone and kidnap their friends, they're going to assume that violence is how to deal with you."

Braelin stepped between them. "They were going to do that next. They wanted to bring you and Nasreen in to examine and test you."

Another of the Firewall guards said sheepishly, "We got a little heavy-handed. We feared that if we politely asked, you would hold back and start asking around. Then the people behind Omega Syndrome would know all about *us.* We're trying to avert much worse violence sponsored by highly insidious forces. Our leadership believes a certain amount of zealotry, you might say, is justified."

Something *cracked* and *crashed* farther back in the station.

Hyde exclaimed, "Fuck! That's probably the 9X guys breaking through."

Nasreen waved at the shuttle. "We can discuss the deep espionage stuff later. For now, we need to get out of here. All of us. The game has changed."

The security officer who'd spoken previously retorted, "That's the problem. There are two more shuttles and more personnel deeper in the other compartments. They weren't prepared to leave and are scrambling to get ready. I've got them on my headset. If Block 9X gets in here, they'll slaughter everyone. We'll need to hold them off."

Braelin rubbed his temples and sighed. "Nothing ain't ever simple, is it?" He looked at his rescuers. "Well, hope you three don't mind turning coat in the middle of a battle."

Dante spun and reloaded his rifle. He had only two magazines left of smart ammo, including the one freshly slapped into the gun, but it might be enough. "Block 9X didn't make much effort to befriend us. I'm sure they'll understand if we repay them for their hospitality."

For once, it was Nasreen's turn to take something literally. "No, they won't understand, Dante. They'll kill us. You said yourself that they're good at what they do. Coming from you, that's quite the compliment."

Hyde crouched and bounded straight up, catching the same railing he'd swung over earlier. "Bullshit!" he spat. "I took down three of their scariest guys. Most of what they have left are the *normal* ones."

Mugoi was watching him and smirked with amusement. "He is truly an impressive specimen, isn't he?"

Dante turned to the apparent leader of Firewall's security. "Give your weapons to our apprentices. We'll hold this point. Get your people onto that shuttle and take off, or if you need to send anyone else to the other ships to help them, do so."

The unit commander looked uncertain at first, but he nodded and directed those of his men still standing to hand their batons to Braelin, Jolo, and Mugoi. Then they picked up their dead and wounded and dragged them into the docked ship through its side door before sealing themselves within.

The one exception was a man who volunteered to aid the others. He headed for a doorway across the bay. It presumably linked to the next compartment where the remaining shuttles awaited.

They exited just in time. The walkway and door above the bay shuddered with the approach of many stomping boots. Dante was sure he heard DeFrieze's mocking, unlovely voice somewhere amid the clamor.

Dante flattened himself against the wall next to the staircase. Block 9X would have the high ground when they came in, but they would also lack the element of surprise. He looked at Mugoi, who was crawling up the railing alongside Hyde.

Dante motioned at the ceiling. A brief, vicious smile split Mugoi's coldly beautiful face, and he jumped straight up, caught some protruding beams and pipes, and crawled along them upside-down.

Hyde looked from the fellow cyborg down at the Marauder, his expression a mashup of wonder and disgust. Dante only shrugged.

Nasreen instructed, "Braelin, Jolo. We trust your abilities, but if all you have are batons, it's probably best that you stay back and guard the ship." She hoisted her stun gun and advanced, ducking behind a small crate platform that provided minimal cover.

Braelin cleared his throat. "I'm gonna have to agree on that."

"Yes," Neburu concurred. "We would be happy to do more. But if they make it to us, they will learn about *everything* we can do."

The door burst open.

Light flashed, and sparks ran all along the walkway, the railing, the walls, and the ceiling. Hyde gritted his teeth as electricity once again half-paralyzed him. He reflexively squeezed the trigger on his smart rifle, dumping an entire magazine into the doorway and against the wall surrounding it.

Dante cursed in silence. The 9Xers had picked up the discarded stun gun used by one of the security guys and deployed it as a room-clearing weapon. Hyde's barrage killed the first one or two men in the group. Someone *thudded* to the floor, and a gloved hand lay over the threshold.

Mugoi was still clinging to the ceiling, also shuddering in pain from the effects of the electric pulse. Somehow, he held on and forced himself to crawl closer to the doorway.

Nasreen steadied her weapon, waiting.

Two men abruptly burst out, one with a grav-shield that deflected the last couple of bullets from Hyde's rifle, the other trying to aim with his stun gun.

Mugoi dropped right onto the second man's head, whacking him with the baton. The impact sent him sailing over the edge of the rail, wailing and sputtering before his head and neck *crunched* against the floor below. The stun gun stayed in Mugoi's hands. He backed up.

Dante bellowed, "Fire!"

Mugoi and Nasreen both launched electric pulses through the doorway. At the same time, Dante used approximate targeting to fire half a magazine in a curved trajectory up the wall and around the corner of the door. The smart rounds could not bend enough mid-flight to pull off the full ninety-degree angle he would have liked, but he riddled the entire far side of the adjacent room with high-speed lead.

Hyde shook off the stun gun's effects, ejected his empty mag, pounded in a new one, and blasted away. Someone beyond the threshold fired a stream of darts at him. One stuck in his elbow, but he ignored it.

Silence. Hyde dropped to one knee, getting out of the line of fire, and Mugoi had pressed himself into the corner perpendicular to the doorway.

DeFrieze's voice rose. "I fuckin' knew you assholes weren't on our side. Nice little display! Too bad we have you cornered in there, and we have other avenues. Stay put. We'll have someone along to deal with you shortly." He let out a sharp yet somehow greasy laugh. Then his men's bootfalls *thudded* away.

Dante was about to order them all through the lower door the Firewall men had left by. Then they all heard the familiar sound of shuttles blasting off close by.

A glance out the bay window confirmed it. Two ships were sailing out into the blackness beyond the substation. Seconds later, flashing lights and alarms announced that the shuttle in their bay was about to launch. Everyone stood aside as it slid into the depressurization safe zone. The gate closed behind it before its thrusters kicked on, propelling it to freedom. The Firewall crew had made it.

Dante exhaled. "Okay, fuck DeFrieze and his friends. We can deal with them some other time. Ambrose! You there? Immediate extraction, please. We're in the bay closest to the main substation."

After about five seconds, the pilot spoke to all of them at once. "I am here, but there's a problem. Your friends in the mercenary company must have planned for some of these guys to get away without telling you about it because they have two gunships hovering out here prepared to shoot them down."

Braelin spun in a half-circle and hurled his baton at the wall, where it crackled and *clanged* to the floor. "Goddammit! Who *are* these sons of bitches?"

Suddenly, Dante was wondering the same thing. He thought he'd known the answer to that question, but Block 9X was a little *too* good and well-funded. He could accept that a paramilitary organization of cons and vets would be capable of ruthless efficiency and would maximize the use of their resources.

For them to have gunships, which were rare outside of Station government forces, suggested they must have had support and sponsorship from someone even more powerful and nefarious than themselves. Dante had a rough idea of who that might be.

"All right," he bellowed. "Change of plans. Now we need to save the shuttles."

Neburu nodded, coldly elegant as always. "Agreed. But how?"

CHAPTER NINETEEN

Hyde headed off any brainstorming sessions with a sobering fact. "Block 9X heard those shuttles take off, and their gunships are probably in communication with them. That means they're going to come back here to deal with *us*."

"Lovely," Mugoi observed. "Alas that the same tricks usually don't work twice. Shall we go after them and have a nice running battle through the halls?"

Nasreen threw her stun gun back over her shoulder on its sling and jogged up the stairs. "No, because we need to get back to the main control room. I thought of a way we can cripple those gunships."

Neburu suggested, "Before crippling them, perhaps we might distract them?"

"Yes," Dante conceded. "Ambrose, I know you hate us, but we don't hate you, okay? So do us a favor and run interference. Buzz around those ships, catch their attention, maybe shoot at them if you can. Or you could get in the escape shuttles' way so they divert course or stay out of the gunships' range. Whatever you can."

The initial response from the headset was a mass of high-pitched mewling, sputtering, coughs, and vague attempts at swearing. "Are you ffffucking crazy?" Ambrose squealed. "I shouldn't be doing this! I should say no! Uggghhhh..."

"Is that a yes?" Dante inquired.

Ambrose raged, "Yes! Now shut up." He went silent. Outside, Dante thought he saw a blur of motion, like a small shuttle with cloaking moving too fast to fully evade detection. Lights flashed as one ship or another opened fire.

Dante nodded. The craft Ambrose piloted was not a military one by any means, but it came equipped with a moderately powerful pulsecore cannon. A lone pilot could operate it crudely and without advanced tracking. Its primary purpose was to repel or destroy asteroids and other space debris or to scare off Dirt-walkers and the like if one crash-landed on Earth. When they'd acquired a ship with that feature, Nasreen had been furious that they'd never done so sooner.

Dante motioned at the door leading back the way they'd come from. "All right. Nasreen, I'll leave it to you. The rest of us will protect you. Let's move."

Hyde and Mugoi went first, fanning out to guard against any circle-backs by DeFrieze's men while the others ascended the stairs and followed them. When everyone was congregated and about to start down the halls, Hyde growled from the rear, "There they are!"

He opened fire with his rifle, emptying another magazine while his companions sprinted down the halls beyond his position. When the gun went silent, he turned and pounded after his friends.

Dante called to him, "How many guys do they have left? How many mags do *you* have left?"

Hyde declared, "We killed about half of their team, so six, maybe seven, not certain. I'm out."

Braelin swore. "Shit. You guys didn't bring a lot of ammo, did you?"

"It's prototype smart ammo, frangible," Dante clarified. "We only had a limited supply to begin with. I've got a little over one more full magazine. Otherwise, we've got Nasreen's stun gun and melee. That will have to be enough."

It helped that 9X did not seem to have any firearms. If they got close enough, their carbon blades would be as deadly as a pulsecore.

They heard their foes approaching through the halls behind them as they came to the shattered remains of the secret door leading into the control room. Dante wondered what DeFrieze had used to breach it or if he had one of the Irondogs rip the thing asunder. Explosives were highly unlikely.

Nasreen rushed to the central console tower. "I'm going to overload the relay," she explained. "Most of these substations can produce a lot of electromagnetic pollution. If they have an adjustable waste vent, we can send that toward the gunships and mess up their steering, comms, and targeting systems, possibly the weapons themselves. They'll be out of commission for a few minutes. Long enough for the shuttles to slip past."

Dante was about to give her the green light, not that she needed it, when the other door leading to the juncture of the diagonal halls and the front of the station burst open.

Hissing through his teeth, Dante raised the smart rifle in time to see four men in the same generic gear worn by the rest of Block 9X piling toward them. All carried sling-guns, the same overpowered pneumatic crossbows that Kali had mentioned selling to their organization. "Down!" he cried, hoping his people would realize he was talking to them.

He and the lead sling-gunner fired at the same time. The smart rifle blazed away. A barrage of seven or eight bullets streaked through the air and ripped the first two men apart, but not before a pair of hard rubber slugs departed the first sling-gun at near-lethal velocity.

Dante reflexively dodged the first, but the second took him in the chest, knocking the wind from his lungs and throwing him off-balance. He stumbled into a side console and fell into a sitting position on one of the chairs used by the late technicians, his chest plate dented but not compromised.

Jolo advanced with Nasreen's stun gun. "Now is not the time to be coy. Overwhelming force would be better." She blasted three pulses into the door where the men had been, spreading them out slightly to cover the widest possible area.

Sparks cracked and popped. Someone howled in pain. When another merc twitched through the doorway, Braelin jumped at him, swatted him in the head with his baton, seized his weapon, and kicked him aside.

"Better." Braelin admired the sling-gun. "Always wanted one of these."

Dante stood. "I saw four. That's two down in that direction, plus however many of DeFrieze's are behind us. The pricks sent a small auxiliary force after us. We've got to assume their backup plans have backup plans."

Nasreen was furiously working away on the central console. "This won't take more than a minute or two. We broke in while they were in the middle of stuff and didn't have time to lock everything down. Not much hacking required."

Then air rushed from the shattered secret door, and something rattled. A compact modern fire extinguisher slid along the floor into the room. Attached to it was a small device that Dante recognized as a pulse cutter—a type of explosive that directed a spear of plasma in one direction, short range only, and relatively safe to use within the Stations as long as no one deployed it against the dome or bulkhead.

"Everyone get down!" he ordered.

Hyde was closest to the extinguisher when the pulse cutter went off. The cyborg turned away from it and dove, but the blast still caught him in the legs and pelvic region, knocking him end over end to the other side of the room. The shockwave also sent

Jolo crashing into Nasreen, disrupting her work, and stunned Mugoi. Dante alone was far enough away to avoid the full effects.

Block 9X, coordinating their movements via a separate comms frequency or by instinct and training, attacked from both directions at once. The two remaining men from the auxiliary team burst through the front door while Svenko the Irondog barged through the destroyed secret entrance.

Dante turned his rifle on the pair of men with sling-guns and emptied it, suppressing the trigger until it clicked. The gun flamed and thundered, and the smart bullets, guided by the internal targeting system and Midas' discretion, found their mark. The first man collapsed in a shower of blood.

The second survived. Two frangible rounds slammed into his chest but failed to penetrate the armor, and another cut open his thigh. He fell to one knee, still holding his gun and now aiming it at Nasreen.

The smart rifle was empty. Dante still had his barely full first mag, but there was no time to reload. He hurled the weapon itself.

The gun struck the surviving auxiliary merc in the arm and shoulder, knocking him sidelong as he fired. Two hard rubber shots zipped over Nasreen's head and ricocheted off the metal of the upper console tower.

Braelin sprang to his feet, aiming his newly acquired sling-gun and squeezing the trigger repeatedly. Rubber balls blasted out, cracking the man's visor and knocking his head into the wall. He finally collapsed.

Meanwhile, on the other side of the room, Mugoi had pounced on Svenko, wrapping his thin yet powerful arms around the larger cyborg's metal neck and trying to take him down via pure technique. What worked easily against a human did not immediately incapacitate a creature of steel and polymer.

Behind the Irondog were the others.

Jolo snatched up the stun gun and fired twice. Electricity

writhed along the metal amid the lingering fumes from the exploded fire extinguisher, and a silhouette of one of the attackers collapsed, convulsing in agony. Someone fired a dart that struck the stun gun, knocking it from her grasp and damaging it to uselessness.

Cursing, Jolo grabbed the baton Mugoi had dropped and moved closer to Nasreen.

Mugoi was now digging his thumbs into Svenko's eye sockets. The Irondog, nearly foam-mouthed with rage, elbowed him furiously and tried to slam himself into the walls to crush Mugoi against his back. The lithe transhuman anticipated the move and flipped over Svenko's shoulders, shoving his head into the metal and knife-handing him in the throat. The Irondog choked and kicked Mugoi in the stomach, knocking him across the room.

When Svenko stood straight again, struggling to see through his damaged artificial eyes, Hyde loomed before him.

"No." Hyde crushed his knee with a single kick. The mechanical leg collapsed and Svenko went down, his brain buzzing with the warnings that replaced natural pain.

Jolo saw her opening and took it. She rushed forward and shoved the baton into the Irondog's opened mouth. The electrical charge surged through the half-metal head and boiled the brain within. Svenko clawed at the air and fell to the floor, a machine that would never work again.

Dante tried to oversee everything at once amid the general chaos. "Ambrose, how's it going? Nasreen, what about you?"

The headset crackled, and through heavy distortion, Ambrose stammered something that sounded like, "...not made for this, shuttles keep trying to get past, they haven't shot them yet, but..."

Dante took that to mean the mission hadn't *failed* yet. It was merely ruining the hell out of Ambrose's day.

Nasreen huffed. "Almost done! Like, twenty seconds." It did sound like the machinery controlled by the substation was whirring and buzzing more than usual. With all the noise of combat, it was hard to be sure.

Suddenly two more men burst into the room from the secret portion of the facility. One of them scored a lucky baton hit against Mugoi's head, causing a brownout that sent the slender cyborg to the floor in a tangle of limbs. Neburu gasped and leapt toward the merc, grappling with him, the baton poised between them.

Braelin rushed in. "I got this! I got this." He was about to throw a punch when Jolo got in the way. Then, when the 9Xer's back was to him, he shrugged and pistoned his fists hard into the man's kidneys and tailbone. It stunned him enough for Neburu to grab his head and snap his neck.

The other intruder was DeFrieze, armed with a carbon-blade baton. He made straight for Hyde. "Come on, you ugly *fuck*," he snarled. "You cheated, you know. I fucking hate cheaters!" Despite his ungainly weight, he was shockingly fast, and Hyde fell back in amazement as two slashes of the ultra-sharp hatchet sheared open parts of his chest and right arm.

DeFrieze was laughing, abandoning whatever professionalism he had in his mad rush for revenge. He swung his weapon wildly, ignoring Nasreen, focused totally on Hyde.

Nasreen slapped the console with an air of finality. "There!"

Machinery shifted, and the light changed as the substation discharged its overloaded energy. It created an artificial storm that spread out through space, a field of electromagnetic chaos aimed straight for the two 9X gunships.

Nasreen pursed her lips in sudden concern. "Um. I hope Ambrose didn't get caught in that."

The sound of a shuttle grew closer, and Dante recognized the rear fin of their ship hovering in the window.

"Time to go." He picked up a fallen baton. "DeFrieze! Catch." He hurled it.

DeFrieze's reflexes were good, Dante had to admit. The oily

man spun and swung his blade-baton at the shock rod. Had he been using any other weapon, it might have deflected the projectile, but the carbon filament knife-edge sheared clean through it. The upper half containing the still-active electrified head struck him in the nose.

"Ahhhh, *fuck*!" he screamed, trembling from the shock.

Hyde grinned at him. "Too bad I don't have a wall to mount your skull on." He reared back with his arm and punched.

The ex-Reaper's massive metal fist sank *into* DeFrieze's chest, crushed most of his ribcage, smashed most of what lay behind it, and lifted the squat man into the air in one motion. Hyde sent him flying back through the devastated secret door with a trail of blood raining through the air as he passed.

Dante barked, "I don't think that's all of them. Get to the front."

As everyone hurried out of the control room, the remaining Block 9X fighters—there couldn't have been more than two or three, but that was still enough to be dangerous—barged in, stepping over the crumpled body of their commander and waving carbon blades of their own. It wouldn't take them long to pick up a projectile weapon from amid all the debris, so Dante ignored them for now in favor of beating a retreat.

The crew ran down the right-hand diagonal corridor, arriving at the substation's front gate at the same time Ambrose's shuttle did. An emergency portal in the crystal hull was mostly for workers doing maintenance in space to get *in*, but the reverse was also true.

Hyde kicked the door open. Immediately there was a sickening change in pressure as air rushed into space. Due to the artificial gravity and residual atmosphere that surrounded the Stations, the effect was not as dangerous here as it would have been out in deeper space, but it still meant that boarding the shuttle would be difficult.

Fortunately, Ambrose continued to prove his worth as a pilot.

He pressed the ship almost directly against the transparent hull, leaving enough room for the bay door to open and create a drawbridge from the substation's walkway to the shuttle's interior.

Ambrose put the craft in a perfectly idle hover pattern. Then, heaving and muttering to himself, he went to the door to toss a zip line out toward his companions. "Hold that, and I'll pull you in."

Behind him, the Firewall's escape craft sailed through the blackness, whole and unharmed, while the gunships idled and struggled to deal with the freak electrical storms that had impaired their systems.

Dante caught the end of the zip line and simply looped it around the base of a lamppost. "Better idea. Everyone hold that thing and pull yourself along. Go."

The apprentices went first, followed by Nasreen. Hyde offered to go last since the final two or three of DeFrieze's men were still approaching, and Hyde would make a better human shield than Dante would.

Dante kept an eye out as he crossed the short expanse, his stomach lurching at the natural discombobulation that always came with even minimal exposure to space, but it was short-lived. He stumbled into the shuttle in time to see Hyde bounding across. One hand clutched the zip line while two men fired sling-guns at his back.

"Ow," Hyde grunted as he rolled into the ship's internal bay. "Those things fucking hurt." The ramp closed behind him.

Ambrose had hastened back to the cockpit. He looked and sounded like he wanted to cry. "Are we done here now? Can we go, finally?"

"Yes," Dante confirmed. The shuttle blasted off, leaving the furious remnant of Block 9X's strike team to watch them go. "Good job, by the way."

As they sailed off, making for anywhere other than Atlantica Central, Dante saw the two gunships barely regaining control of themselves. They had been drifting in such a way that they were about to collide, but one of them regained function in time to steer away, only grazing the other and knocking loose a few pieces of external plating. It was beautiful to see.

Braelin whistled as everyone clutched at whatever fastened-down objects they could find to hold onto. There was no time to strap themselves into seats per the usual protocol. "Dunno about the rest of you, but I think I need about thirty-seven beers."

Jolo suggested with a straight face, "Thirty-eight, preferably."

CHAPTER TWENTY

Dante Shale was not a particularly emotional man by nature. Sitting in the corner of Nasreen's safehouse, surveying everything and everyone before him, it was obvious that the present moment was an exception.

He felt things the way most people did much of the time, but he had tamed and disciplined his feelings long ago. Sometimes he wondered if he did not experience emotional turmoil to the same extent as the average person.

On the occasions when an inner signal nearly overwhelmed him, whether it was passion, revulsion, or deep contemplative neutrality, it baffled him. He had no words for how to express it to himself or anyone else.

Looking over the crowded space and all the people within it, he supposed that the best term for what swelled within him was simply *relief*. The nightmare was over, and everyone was safely back together. That was the essence of it.

There was more to it than that. He would need more time to figure out how to articulate it. Such things were not his specialty.

Amid the chatter, banter, and laughter, someone—either Braelin or Ambrose, Dante couldn't see around a potted plant well enough to be certain—squeezed too close to Hyde and jostled against him.

"*Hey!*" The big cyborg's gruff bellow rang out, drowning out the other sounds. "Watch it. No, it's fine. I'm kidding, *amigo*. This is your warning not to do that in the field or when I'm in a bad mood. When it's a time and place like this, we'll say it's okay. Heh, heh."

Braelin replied, "Whoops! Well then, point taken, friend. Usually, I pride myself on being a little more careful, but I have had a drink or two and I ain't used to crowded quarters like this, especially not with a man of your, erm, size."

Neburu chimed in, "It is true. Braelin is short enough that he can usually duck between most people's legs." Her smile was good-natured and teasing. As was often the case with her, Dante wondered if she were simply leading Klement on for reasons of professional harmony.

Braelin spun and leveled an index finger at her. "Watch your mouth. Ah, who am I kidding? It's true. I get around that way all the time, crawling along the floor and slipping between everyone's legs. Kind of convenient when you think about it."

Mugoi's low, dry chuckle floated up from where he lounged rather like a cat on the backrest of Nasreen's couch. "I suppose I could do the same. Undignified, yes, but efficient. I will have to practice it at the next opportunity."

Nasreen sat on the couch in front of him. She pushed him, and he rolled off, somehow landing on his feet. "Oh, stop it, Mugoi. Everything isn't a competition, you know. It was only a joke."

"How do you know I wasn't joking, too?"

Nasreen shrugged.

Ambrose sat close to Dante, nursing a bottle of rice beer. "Well, we are all in one piece, which is the most important thing. I did not want to leave any pieces of myself in Atlantica Central before heading back to Earth, I must say. Which is something I look forward to doing very soon."

His contented smile faded, and he frowned. "Although I am without a shuttle of my own."

Dante patted his shoulder. "We'll give you one. Not one of the *best* ones, but good enough to get you Dirtside and back in business down there. On one condition, which I'm sure you can guess."

He exhaled and looked off to the side. "That I must be your getaway pilot again if you need it?"

"Exactly." Dante took a swig of his beer. "You're the best, after all."

Then it clicked. The mishmash of emotions—the foreign territory of human feelings—sharpened in focus, and he understood it at last.

This small, fortified apartment was never supposed to house so many people. Nasreen had intended it for herself and perhaps one extra person. Seven of them would all be in each other's way and stepping on one another's feet for the duration of their mutual stay. That wasn't important.

What *was* important was that nobody minded right now. They belonged together, even if it was only a temporary and awkward arrangement. Seeing them all healthy, free, and getting along soothed and filled his heart in a way he never would have expected and could not have understood until it happened at last.

He recalled what Nasreen had said earlier. She felt almost like a parent to the three they'd taken under their wings. It had sounded ridiculous at first, but he was rapidly modifying his perceptions.

It was unlikely he'd admit it to anyone else. He had acknowledged it. He knew what she meant. These people were his family, his responsibility. Something above and outside of himself placed a wholly natural and healthy pressure on him to see them protected and cared for. The fact of their abduction had been eating away at him since it had happened.

Now it was over, and they were back.

"Sir," Midas offered, in a gentle tone that was not as annoying as Dante might have thought. *"It is okay, you know. You are allowed to be* happy. *As I understand it, this is one of the, if not* the *most important of all human traits."*

He smiled, partially in wry amusement. "Sure. Thanks. I guess I needed to hear that from an outside observer."

Ambrose looked at him sidelong, then shook his head when he realized Dante was speaking to someone else.

Their communal reverie could not last forever.

Jolo Neburu was the first to get them back to business. "Excuse me. We must discuss Firewall. After what happened back there, they will have no way of knowing why we acted as we did unless we contact them and make peace."

Nasreen pointed out, "They were the ones who abducted you and held you against your will, so I would say we're even. But yes, it's a matter that will require some diplomacy, and sooner rather than later."

Braelin added, "Well, they convinced us. I know, Stockholm Syndrome and all that, but they're right. They really are. Those Voices, this Omega Syndrome, is real and someone has to fight it."

Neburu's response was swift. "Of course. We are in agreement. Unfortunately, the rescue operation involved several persons in this room killing Firewall personnel. Even if they can acknowledge that we all helped cover the escape of their ships, they may not think kindly enough of us to overlook the deaths of their operatives."

Dante grimaced. That had occurred to him, and he'd wanted to avoid it. They would need to deal with it.

Nasreen offered, "We could reach out at once if we knew how. They are not easy to find."

Mugoi stretched his glistening limbs and moved closer to the center of the room. "Early on, I gained access to a comm-shiv."

Dante was not familiar with comm-shivs. They were a fairly new technology based on an older device before his time. He grasped that they were small, insertable spike-like or knife-like things that contained data and allowed messages to be relayed.

The sleek being went on, "I had hopes that it would at least allow those who found my body to go after those who took us if it came to that. Now we could use it to back-trace a communication line to Firewall, assuming they haven't yet burned all old connections."

Nasreen mentioned, "They may. I would, in their position, but they might have other priorities first."

Hyde growled. "I hate shit like this. Doing that could open us up to trackers. Then this little safehouse wouldn't be so safe. Firewall wouldn't even have to deal with us themselves. They could send the info to Block 9X, who'd be happy to put a gunship outside our window in short order."

Heavy silence descended on the apartment. Everyone looked at Dante.

He hesitated, more conflicted than usual. His apprentices, his wards…he wanted to protect them from needless harm no matter what. Being overprotective would stunt their development. For them to grow stronger and wiser, they would need him to trust them to know what they were talking about some of the time and allow them a degree of responsibility.

He drew a deep breath. "Yes. Run the trace, Mugoi, and send the message that in this situation, the enemy of our enemy is our friend."

Mugoi's perfect, androgynous face mimicked a raised eyebrow look of concern. "If you insist."

"I do." Dante stood. "I trust you. It's better than inaction. Do it…and let the chips fall where they may."

AUTHOR NOTES MICHAEL ANDERLE

AUGUST 9, 2022

Thank you for not only reading this story with these author notes as well.

Have you ever wondered what it would be like to live just outside Earth's atmosphere?

For me, near-Earth orbit (NEO) has been a fascination for a long time.

I don't think I would want to go up now, with the minimal amount of support and infrastructure we have at the present space station. However, I would love to live on a space station that is effectively a huge set of hotels hanging out in space.

Which is part of the reason I enjoy creating series such as this one.

Presently, most individuals who are reading this book could, in one way or another, find their way onto a plane and, if they have a passport, get to another area in the world within eighteen hours once the plane takes off.

The only concern you have to have is whether that plane decompresses or falls out of the sky.

Sometimes having an active imagination REALLY SUCKS when taking off or landing. Lots of "Oh, shit, this could go wrong right about now!"

You don't usually have to worry about whether where you land might implode and kill everyone.

My imagination is part of what keeps me from going up, or wishing to go up, to the stations up in the outer atmosphere now.

In the far future, when large space stations exist and pepper the skies around our Earth, one would like to think humanity has figured out a way to live peacefully and co-exist without causing problems for those living in the firmament of space.

However, as I've mentioned in other author notes, I'm cynical and don't see it happening.

I do think, however, that with everybody having to be careful with the space stations, some agreement about what you can and *cannot* do on space stations would have to be agreed to, where the death penalty would be implemented the same across every one of them.

For example, "No one shoots something that can go through walls!"

That one seems obvious, right?

If even competing groups of humans can't universally agree to a rule like that, what hope do we have for building infrastructure in space anyway?

It's almost like we would have another opportunity to build the Ten Commandments and have all of us agree to it. If nothing else, anyone in space needs to respect the option of imminent death that can kill everyone.

I'm going to be fifty-five this year, so I really doubt I will see the future in *Hellcat:* humanity building massive space stations in outer space and moving from one to another as if we were flying from New York to London.

I hope you have enjoyed this new series in the *Atlantica* universe. If you didn't catch our first four trilogies that talk about Atlantica before the world collapsed, go check them out here:

Atlantica: John Chambers

Atlantica: Valentina Winters

Atlantica: Terra Kris

Atlantica: Santana Sokolov

I look forward to talking to you in the next book!

Ad Aeternitatem,

Michael Anderle

MORE STORIES with Michael newsletter HERE:
https://michael.beehiiv.com/

OTHER ATLANTICA BOOKS

John Chambers Books

Her Mother's Pendant (Book 1)

The Mystery Deepens (Book 2)

One Last Choice (Book 3)

Valentina Winters

The Red Countess (Book 1)

One Night to Kill (Book 2)

One Death Too Few (Book 3)

Terra Kris

She is the Law (Book 1)

Law or Justice (Book 2)

Justice Served (Book 3)

Santana Sokolov

Law of the Jungle (Book 1)

Inner City Jungle (coming soon)

Rumble in the Jungle (coming soon)

Justice Begins

The First Executioner

Aiming Blind

High Lead and Low Deeds

No Backing Down

Justice is Not Blind

Scorched Earth

BOOKS BY MICHAEL ANDERLE

Sign up for the LMBPN email list to be notified of new releases and special deals!

https://lmbpn.com/email/

For a complete list of books by Michael Anderle, please visit:

www.lmbpn.com/ma-books/